"Let me up!"
Robyn demanded

She tried to push him away from her.

"Not yet," Jared returned huskily, trailing his knuckles across her mouth. His thumb followed and parted her lips. He stroked the curve of her teeth, then her tongue.

"So cold on the outside," he murmured, "and so warm within. You know, what my father said about you, that you were as dried up as an old maid, isn't true."

Robyn gasped, shocked and hurt. "He said that?" And then she caught her breath instinctively as Jared suddenly brought his mouth to hers.

How could she have forgotten what it was like to be kissed by him? How helpless he made her feel! How impossible it was to fight him!

ANNE MATHER began her career by writing the kind of book she likes to read—romance. Married, with two teenage children, this northern England author has become a favorite with readers of romance fiction the world over—her books have been translated into many languages and are read in countless countries. Since her first novel was published in 1970, Anne Mather has written more than eighty romances, with over ninety million copies sold!

Books by Anne Mather

STORMSPELL
WILD CONCERTO
HIDDEN IN THE FLAME
THE LONGEST PLEASURE

HARLEQUIN PRESENTS
810—ACT OF POSSESSION
843—STOLEN SUMMER
869—PALE ORCHID
899—AN ALL-CONSUMING PASSION
1003—NIGHT HEAT
1044—BURNING INHERITANCE

HARLEQUIN ROMANCE
1631—MASQUERADE
1656—AUTUMN OF THE WITCH

Don't miss any of our special offers. Write to us at the following address for information on our newest releases.

Harlequin Reader Service
901 Fuhrmann Blvd., P.O. Box 1397, Buffalo, NY 14240
Canadian address: P.O. Box 603,
Fort Erie, Ont. L2A 5X3

ANNE MATHER

trial of innocence

Harlequin Books

TORONTO • NEW YORK • LONDON
AMSTERDAM • PARIS • SYDNEY • HAMBURG
STOCKHOLM • ATHENS • TOKYO • MILAN

Harlequin Presents first edition November 1988
ISBN 0-373-11122-3

Original hardcover edition published in 1988
by Mills & Boon Limited

CHAPTER ONE

SHE shouldn't have come to the airport. She hadn't wanted to come, goodness knew, but Ben had been so adamant, and she hadn't been able to think of a single legitimate reason why she should not want to meet Stephen's brother after all these years. After all, the rest of the household was in an uproar in anticipation of his return and, after the traumatic events of the past few weeks, she, like them, should have been looking forward to such a happy event. Ben was. In spite of the animosity which had existed between him and his younger son for so long—an animosity which Robyn couldn't help feeling responsible for—he was awaiting Jared's return with an almost painful intensity, looking to his younger son to heal the wounds left by Stephen's death.

For her part, Robyn felt as if she had been living in a vacuum ever since the police inspector arrived to inform them of Stephen's accident. At first, she had experienced a sense of unreality, a lack of belief in what he was saying; and then, an almost shameful feeling of relief that Stephen was dead, that their marriage was over, that never again would she have to suffer the pain and humiliation that Stephen's many defections had caused her.

Of course, his father had known what Stephen was like, but he had been prepared to overlook his elder son's imperfections. He had always loved Stephen best, and although it had angered him when Jared went away, he had not really cared. Perhaps Stephen and his father had been alike, Robyn reflected now. More alike than she knew, anyway. Certainly, Ben's second wife—the mother of his younger son—had not found their marriage tenable. Ben had divorced her for desertion when Jared was only five years old, and although, when she first got to know him, Robyn had sympathised with her father-in-law, her experiences with Stephen had made her wonder whether his father had been as completely innocent as he maintained.

Still, that particular skeleton had never significantly raised its ugly head. Perhaps because he liked her, perhaps because she was the girl he had wanted Stephen to marry, Ben had always been excessively kind to Robyn, and she had to admit, she had come to rely on his support in recent years. In fact, she had sometimes felt that she and Ben had more in common than she and Stephen ever had, and he had certainly done his best to ease the situation between them.

But that was all in the past now. Stephen was dead and, instead of dwelling on his shortcomings, she should be mourning his loss. He had been her husband for the past eight years, after all, and he was Daniel's father. She had to remember that, and forget everything else.

None the less, this duty she had to perform today, this coming to London airport to welcome home the prodigal son, was not one she cherished. On the contrary, she had done everything she could to avoid the responsibility, even to the extent of inventing a headache this morning in the hope that Ben would take pity on her and send someone else in her place.

But he hadn't. He had been adamant. 'One of us should be there, Robyn,' he had said quietly. 'And as I can't...'

The reminder of the stroke which had crippled him three years ago and left Stephen in control of the family business was enough to remind Robyn of her continued dependence on him. For Daniel's sake, she had to go; for Daniel's sake, she had to forget the past.

All the same, she had been in a state of some agitation all the way down on the M1, and she was sure that, had she been driving herself, she would never have found the way to Heathrow. It was just as well that David McCloud, her father-in-law's chauffeur, had been at the wheel, and Robyn had been able to sit back and pretend that her thoughts were as placid as his.

Daniel had wanted to come with her. He was very excited about the arrival of this long-absent uncle, of whom he had latterly heard so much. 'How far away is Australia?' he had asked, not once, but a dozen times, making his grandfather produce an atlas of the world to show him exactly where his father's brother had been living for the past six years. 'But why haven't I ever seen him?' he had persisted to his mother, after his grandfather had failed to produce a satisfactory answer. 'Why has he never come here for a holiday? Saddlebridge is his home, too, isn't it? Grandpa says it is, but he won't say why Uncle Jared went away.'

'It's a long story,' Robyn had replied briskly, hoping Daniel's propensity for asking personal questions was not going to be too much of a problem. It was what came of being the only child in a household of adults, all of whom had their own reasons for spoiling him. He was at times impertinent and precocious, and he was growing up with the impression that he was the most important member of the household. He had needed a father, she thought now. The trouble was, Stephen had been at home so rarely, he had never fulfilled that role.

'I like long stories,' Daniel had protested, when Robyn had proved as unforthcoming as his grandfather. 'Well, if you won't tell me, I'm going to ask Uncle Jared when he gets here. I bet he won't mind talking about it. I bet it's because of some dumb row he had with Grandpa before he went away.'

Yes, entirely too precocious, Robyn reflected bitterly, wondering what she had ever done to deserve this new threat to her peace of mind. She had been a good wife; too good, some people might say, who didn't know her reasons for making herself the kind of wife Stephen had wanted. Some of her friends had thought she was mad to put up with his behaviour, had considered her contention that Daniel needed both his parents to be both untrue and outdated. But Robyn had been determined that Daniel should not be deprived of the heritage that was his, and if she had sometimes wanted to scream with frustration and rebel, thankfully those times had been becoming fewer. After all, she was thirty-two now, no longer a foolish girl to whom the prospect of a loveless marriage offered any fears. She had learned that habit and convenience were far more comfortable bedfellows than the grand passion written about in the kind of books so popular in Saddleford Public Library. In spite of everything, she had made a home for herself at Saddlebridge, and since Ben's incapacitation she had become both his nurse and his confidante. With Stephen's death, she had briefly believed she might have a future, after all. And then Ben had told her he had sent for Jared; that Stephen's death had altered everything; and Robyn had realised how wrong she had been.

Now, standing outside the Customs hall, waiting for the passengers from the Qantas flight to clear Immigration, Robyn steeled herself for the ordeal of facing Jared again after all this time. How long had it been? she wondered, pretending she needed to think about her answer. She knew exactly how long it was since Jared had paid his last visit to Saddlebridge. It was six years and four months, give or take a few days. In the July, just after he had graduated from university. She and Stephen had been married more than two years, and Daniel had been almost eighteen months old.

She caught her lower lip between her teeth and bit, hard. She was doing it again, she thought irritably. Dwelling on the past, and allowing prior events to colour her mood. She had to stop it. Just because her life had altered little since he went away, it was no reason to view this coming meeting with unnecessary trepidation. It was foolish to imagine Jared would not have changed. Heavens, when he went away he had been little more than a boy, with no experience of life to speak of. Now, after six years of being independent, of working at a variety of jobs, from sheep-shearing in New South Wales to working in a hotel in Queensland, he had to have changed out of all recognition. He probably hadn't given a thought to his family for years, and his father's letter must have been a bolt from the blue.

They had learned, from the reply he had sent to his father, that for the past two years he had been working for a firm of financial consultants in Sydney. Evidently, he had grown tired of manual labour, and decided to use the qualifications he had earned at university at last. In any event, he had agreed to come home, although he had made no promises about how long he might stay, and Robyn suspected that taking over his dead brother's position as managing director of Morley Textiles might seem very mundane after the life he was used to.

Or was that just wishful thinking? she asked herself uneasily, aware that, in this instance, her desires conflicted with those of her father-in-law. All the same, although Jared had expressed his grief at the news of his brother's death, he had not mentioned the business at all. And Ben should know that just because he wanted—*expected*—Jared to stay was no reason to assume he would.

Robyn looked around now, wishing McCloud was with her. She felt conspicuously obvious standing here, and she hoped Jared would not think she had arranged this situation. But parking at the airport was not easy, and the chauffeur had suggested it might be simpler if he stayed with the car, so that the effort of hefting Jared's luggage to some distance parking place would not prove a problem.

The passengers from a recently landed transatlantic flight were gradually dispersing, and the first trickle of Australian passengers was beginning to filter through. Watching the smiling, suntanned faces as they were greeted by friends and relatives, Robyn decided she could tell who were from Oz and who were not. Australians looked more relaxed somehow, she thought, watching a middle-aged couple embracing a family group that included two small children, scarcely out of nappies. But then, her sense of satisfaction was ruined by a distinctly mid-western drawl, and that particular attempt at self-distraction was defeated.

Sighing, she slipped the strap of her bag over one shoulder, and thrust her hands into the pockets of her purple corded jacket. Her nerves were stretching by the minute, and, although earlier in the day she had convinced herself she didn't care what she looked like or what Jared might think of her, the continued delay was wearing. Catching a glimpse of her reflection in the glass wall opposite, she saw that the coil of hair at her nape was shedding black strands on to her collar, and that the cup of coffee and the sandwich, which she and McCloud had shared at a motorway service area, had removed all trace of lipstick from her mouth. She looked pale and tired, she thought resignedly, used to her unremarkable features, and seeing no charm in them. She hoped Jared would imagine she was grieving over Stephen's sudden demise. How disgusted he would be if he guessed how difficult it was for her to mourn her husband's passing.

'Hello, Robyn!'

She had not heard him approach, had been too absorbed in her own reflection to notice the tall, lean man, in cream cotton trousers and a dark brown suede jerkin, detach himself from the group of arriving passengers and make his way towards her. Her first intimation that she was no longer alone was when he spoke to her, and she started violently at the amazingly familiar tones.

'Jared!' she got out through dry lips, aware that, for all her preparations, she had not been prepared for this moment. 'Well...how nice to see you. You—you look well. Did you have a good journey?'

'Well...I did,' he mocked gently, setting down the overnight bag he was carrying and glancing round. 'Don't tell me you're all the welcoming party there is. Where's Dad? Didn't he come with you?'

'We—er—we thought it would be too much for him,' Robyn stammered awkwardly, trying not to stare at him too obviously. She had been right in her speculation. He *had* changed. This cool-eyed stranger was nothing like the rebellious youth who had left the country. Recognisable he might be, but familiar he was not.

'Too much for him?' echoed Jared drily, the inflection in his tone evidence of his scepticism. 'That's an original excuse, anyway.' He ran a careless hand over the silky sun-streaked hair that lapped his collar. 'So—you pulled the short straw, hmm? Poor Robyn! I bet this was one duty you could have done without.'

Robyn squared her shoulders, refusing to let him see that he was disconcerting her. 'Not at all,' she replied politely, if not altogether truthfully. 'It's good to see you again, Jared. You've—matured. I'd hardly have recognised you.'

It wasn't true, but he couldn't know that, although his grey-green eyes did register a certain cynicism at her remarks. 'I wasn't a boy when I went away, Robyn,' he said, his eyes shifting to some point beyond her head. 'But you know that, don't you? In spite of your pleas to the contrary.'

Robyn started to say, I don't know what you mean, and then changed it to, 'I don't know—exactly where Mr McCloud is. Is this all your luggage?' She indicated the medium-sized suitcase he had set down at his feet. 'We thought you'd have more.'

'For a week's stay?' Jared shrugged, bending to possess himself of the suitcase once again. 'I travel light, Robyn. I find it's the best way.'

Robyn swallowed. 'A—a *week's* stay?'

'Give or take a day or so. Holidaying in England in winter, when it's summer down under, doesn't exactly appeal to me.'

'Holidaying?' Robyn licked her lips. 'But I thought——'

She broke off abruptly, but Jared raised a speculative eyebrow. 'Yes? You thought—what? That I was staying longer, obviously. Now, why should you think that, I wonder?'

Robyn shook her head. 'Well—well, I assumed——'

'I think this is where I came in,' said Jared briefly. 'Come on. Let's find Mac, shall we? We can talk in the car. I presume you did come down by car, didn't you? Or has the old man invested in a helicopter?'

'I doubt if your father could afford to invest in a helicopter,' retorted Robyn stiffly, walking at his side as they crossed the arrivals lounge to emerge into the cold crisp air of a November morning. For once, the sun was shining, and its brilliance gave the coldly practical airport buildings an unexpected warmth. 'Oh, there's the car.' She raised her arm to wave. 'Mr McCloud! We're over here.'

'Still the same old Roller,' commented Jared satirically, as the chauffeur guided the elderly Rolls-Royce in their direction, but Robyn chose not to bite. He could be as sarcastic as he liked, she told herself fiercely. She wasn't going to defend his father to him. If he wanted to make fun of a sick old man, that was his affair. She would not condone it by making excuses.

David McCloud's welcome more than made up for any lack of enthusiasm on her part. 'It's good to have you back, Jared,' he exclaimed, shaking the younger man's hand warmly with both of his. 'We've missed you, the missus and me. Saddlebridge hasn't been the same since you went away.'

'It's good to see you, Mac,' returned Jared easily, with more warmth in his voice than he had shown thus far. 'How is Janet? And the boys? I guess Jamie must be working by now.'

'Ay, he's teaching in Nottingham just now,' replied Mac, with evident pride, stowing Jared's suitcase in the capacious boot of the car as he spoke. 'Donald's still at school, of course, but we hear he's doing very nicely.'

Jared expressed his admiration as he opened the rear door of the limousine for Robyn to get in. Although she resented the feeling that she was being patronised, Robyn made no demur. It would be less harrowing if Jared sat up front with the chauffeur, even if she had come to regard that position as her own.

However, to her surprise—and consternation—Jared did not take the front seat. Instead, he climbed into the back of the car with her, closing the door and joining her on the worn leather banquette.

'You look as if you're doing very nicely yourself, Jared,' Mac declared, taking his seat behind the wheel. 'Wait until Janet sees that tan. Och, she'll be green with envy!'

Jared leant forward then to make some inaudible comment—inaudible to Robyn, anyway—and both men laughed. Robyn found she was gritting her teeth. She had forgotten how popular Jared had always been with the staff at Saddlebridge; had forgotten his propensity for getting under people's skins—particularly hers.

The amount of traffic waiting to get out of the airport's perimeter required all McCloud's attention, and Robyn tensed as Jared relaxed beside her. In spite of her unwanted resentment at his evident preference for the chauffeur's company, she was apprehensive of what he might unthinkingly reveal, and although McCloud was occupied, he was not deaf.

'So...' Jared murmured, attracting her attention, 'do you want to talk about it?'

Robyn swallowed. 'Stephen's accident?'

'What else?'

What else, indeed? Robyn licked her lips. 'Didn't your father tell you?'

Jared shrugged, his shoulders depressing the soft leather. 'He wrote that Steve's car went over the bridge at Carnthwaite. Is that all there was to it? When did it happen?'

Robyn shifted a little uncomfortably. 'Surely he told you. It happened six weeks ago——'

'That wasn't what I meant.' Grey-green eyes, shaded by sun-bleached lashes, several shades darker than his hair, narrowed perceptibly. 'What time of *day* did it happen? Dad never said.'

Robyn suspected he knew what the answer must be, and with McCloud sitting up front, hearing every word that was said, she could hardly prevaricate. 'I—it was evening,' she said, hoping he would be satisfied with that. 'Unfortunately, he wasn't found until early the next morning. It was raining pretty heavily. No one saw the car leave the road.'

Jared made a sound of disbelief. 'But surely there must have been some evidence of what had happened. Wasn't the bridge damaged in any way?'

Of course it had been. Aware of McCloud's sympathetic gaze through the rear-view mirror, Robyn strove to avoid the damning revelation that few people used Carnthwaite bridge at one o'clock in the morning.

'It was raining,' she repeated, assuming an interest in a plane that was taking off overhead. 'I expect your father will give you all the details.'

Jared made no comment at this, and for a short time Robyn breathed a little more easily. If she could just get this journey over, she thought encouragingly. Once they reached Saddlebridge, she could at least avoid his presence.

Even so, his silence did promote an awareness of him she would rather not have experienced. While they were talking, she had needed all her concentration to evade his questions, but now that that particular obstacle had been overcome, she was left with her unwelcome sensitivity to his nearness. It was incredible that even after so many years she should still feel that mawkish awareness of something that was long since dead. That particular incident in her past should hold no attraction for her, and she despised herself utterly for allowing it to intrude on what should have been her grief.

All the same, it was impossible not to be conscious of the man beside her. It was natural enough that she should notice the changes in him, and she was quite sure he was not ignorant of his own attraction to the opposite sex. After all, girls had hung around Jared for as long as she could remember. There had always been some girl phoning him up or coming to the house to see him. Even when they were children, when Stephen was fifteen,

Robyn fourteen, and Jared a precocious nine, he had always had some girl in tow—albeit without any effort on his part. Maybe that was why Stephen had resented him so much, and why Ben had always felt the need to protect his elder son.

She sighed. If only it had been that simple. Ben's aversion to his younger son went deeper than that. That was why she had been so shocked when she learned Ben had sent for Jared. It was the last thing she had expected him to do. The last thing she had *wanted* him to do.

But he was here now, and there was nothing she could do about it. After six years of convincing herself that she was unlikely ever to see Jared again, he had come back, and that was something she was going to have to live with.

Catching her breath, she permitted herself a sidelong glance in his direction. To her relief, he was looking out of the window of the car, and she was able to observe him without his knowledge. He hadn't changed that much, not really, she realised tensely. Oh, he was older— weren't they all?—but his features were not that different from when he went away. His face was less angular, perhaps. He had been very thin when he went away, whereas now his features were lean, but not so finely drawn. His skin was darker, too, with the tan McCloud had admired earlier, but the narrow cheekbones and thin-lipped mouth were as she remembered them, and only experience deepened the narrowed penetration of his eyes.

And then he turned his head and looked at her, and her composure fled. Just for an instant, he looked at her without the guarded expression he had worn since he'd got off the plane, and her breathing became constricted. Dear God, she thought in alarm, he hasn't forgotten anything. And that knowledge was more frightening than anything else.

She looked away at once, hoping he had not glimpsed the panic in her eyes, but his next words set her teeth on edge. 'How is Daniel?' he enquired smoothly, his voice devoid of all emotion. 'He must be what? Seven now? Eight?'

'He's seven,' said Robyn quickly, hoping to evade any further questions about Daniel by changing the subject. 'Um—you must be tired. If you want to sleep, don't let me stop you.'

Jared's lips twisted. 'How kind. But I'm fine, really. I slept on the plane. There wasn't much else to do.'

Robyn forced a tight smile. 'I wouldn't know. I've never travelled so far myself.'

'No.' Jared inclined his head. 'No, you wouldn't, would you?'

Robyn swallowed, casting a meaningful glance in the chauffeur's direction. 'I'm probably not the travelling kind.'

'No.' Jared conceded the point. 'You always did like Saddlebridge best.'

Robyn bent her head. 'Saddlebridge is my home. You know that.'

'Do I ever,' jeered Jared mockingly. And then, 'So tell me about yourself, about what you do all day; about Daniel.'

Robyn took a deep breath. 'What can I tell you that you don't already know? Things don't change at Saddlebridge. Not significantly, anyway. Although, since your father had his stroke——'

'His *what*?'

Jared halted her there, a lean brown hand gripping her arm in sudden violence. 'Did you say—stroke?'

'Yes.' Robyn nodded in confusion. 'But you knew——'

'Like hell I did!' he snarled savagely. 'When was this? Before or after Steve's accident?'

Robyn stared at him. 'Be—before, of course,' she stammered blankly. 'Quite a bit before. Er—about three years, I suppose.'

'Three years!' Jared gazed at her, aghast. 'For Christ's sake, why wasn't I told at the time?'

Robyn winced as his strong fingers dug into her flesh, even through the thickness of her sleeve. 'I thought you had been,' she protested faintly. 'Didn't Stephen write to you?'

'Stephen?' Jared's jaw hardened. 'No. Nobody wrote to me. The first communication I had from England was from my father, telling me that Steve was dead.'

Robyn didn't know what to say. 'I—I'm sorry.'

'Yes. So am I.' Jared seemed to realise he was hurting her and abruptly let her go. 'My God! So that was what you meant when you said the old man wasn't fit enough to come to the airport. And I thought he must have had second thoughts about sending for me.'

'Oh, no.' Robin shook her head. 'He—he's looking forward to seeing you. Since—well, since the funeral, he's talked of little else.'

'Really?' Jared did not sound convinced. 'So how is he now?'

'Irascible.' Robyn tried to speak lightly. 'He's—partially paralysed. His speech may be imperfect, but his brain's as sharp as ever.'

Jared frowned. 'And who's running the mill now that—Steve's not around?'

'Um—well, I am,' admitted Robyn unwillingly. 'At least, I deliver your father's orders to Frank Beasley and Maurice Woodhouse.'

'Maurice Woodhouse! Is he still there?' Jared made an evident effort to relax again, lying back in the seat beside her and fixing her with an unnerving stare. 'My God, I'm beginning to understand. That's why I've been summoned to the presence, isn't it? The old man thinks he can persuade me to take Steve's place. The prince is dead, long live the prince, hmm?'

Robyn moistened her lips. 'You'll have to ask him that,' she said, conscious that McCloud could hear every word that was said. He must know she was avoiding a direct answer, but it couldn't be helped. It was up to Ben to put his case himself; not her.

Jared shifted to rest an ankle across his knee, gazing somewhat broodingly at his fingers, plucking at the laces of his suede boot. 'Did you go along with this?' he asked suddenly, and Robyn expelled her breath unsteadily.

'I—um—it was your father's decision, not mine,' she murmured uneasily, wishing she had known he was unaware of his father's condition. Had Ben been aware of his son's ignorance? she wondered frustratedly. Had he banked on the certainty that sooner or later she would betray the truth?

'That's not what I asked,' Jared was saying now, turning cool, calculating eyes in her direction. 'I asked if you went along with it? Did you? *Do* you?'

Robyn put up a nervous hand and looped an untidy strand of hair behind her ear. 'If it's what your father wants...' she murmured awkwardly, and avoided his eyes.

'Is that a yes or a no?'

Robyn sighed. 'Jared, Saddlebridge is as much your home as mine.'

'How diplomatic!' His lips twisted. 'Did you learn that from Steve or my father?'

'Jared——'

'You've not found yourself a wife then, Jared?'

McCloud's sudden intervention came as a welcome escape, and Robyn's grateful eyes sought the chauffeur's in the mirror.

'No.' Jared's response was ironic. 'Not yet, Mac. I've not been as lucky as you. The women I choose invariably prefer someone else.'

'The *women* you choose.' McCloud took him up on his words. 'That sounds like there have been quite a number.'

'A few,' agreed Jared carelessly, and Robyn felt a painful tightening of her stomach muscles. Yet, why should it surprise her that Jared had had other women? It had always been so. She knew that.

'Well, you don't sound too heartbroken,' remarked McCloud drily. 'I'd guess there are a few ladies around

Saddleford who won't be sorry to find you're still unattached.'

Jared smiled, but he made no comment, and Robyn wondered what he was thinking. There was no doubt his return to Saddlebridge—however brief that return might be—would attract a certain amount of attention. And there were several young women, women younger than herself, who would be more than willing to welcome him back. Robyn felt suddenly very old.

And, as if noticing how strained she had become, Jared seemed to take pity on her. 'You know,' he said, and although she tensed at his words, he was settling back in his seat as he spoke, 'I think I will try and doze, after all. You don't mind, do you, Robyn? I'd like to be wide awake when I meet the old man.'

CHAPTER TWO

IT WAS just after half-past eight the next morning when Robyn turned the Ford estate car between the gates of Morley Textiles. Parking in the space reserved for the managing director, she uncoiled herself from behind the wheel, and made a determined effort to act naturally as she walked across the cobbled yard to the office block. There were bound to be faces looking out of windows, wondering how she was going to react now that Jared had come back, speculating about her, and Daniel's, position, now that the younger son was evidently to inherit his father's business, and she had no wish to feed their curiosity.

If only that was all she had to worry about, she thought drily, mounting the external wooden staircase to her office. Whether or not Jared chose to take up Ben's offer was immaterial to her. The insurance Stephen had left would ensure Daniel's future was secure, and that was all she cared about.

All the same, she was aware that convincing the staff of the fact was another matter altogether, and she was quite prepared for the divisions of loyalty any change of status would bring.

Meanwhile, she had a business to run, and it wasn't easy to concentrate on that while her thoughts continued to dwell on what might be happening at the house. She couldn't forget that Daniel had shown a disturbing fascination for his uncle's company the night before, and that although Mr McCloud would be taking him to school shortly, he had just been sitting down to his breakfast when she left. Of course, Jared was not up yet, and there was every likelihood that he wouldn't be

20

before Daniel left the house, but he could be; he *could* be.

Entering the office which Ben Morley had used until his stroke, Robyn firmly put all thoughts of Jared—and Daniel—aside, and shed her tweed jacket on to the old-fashioned coat-stand that stood just inside the door. She saw, with some gratitude, that Mr Matthews, the caretaker, had lit the fire for her arrival, and already its crackling warmth was banishing the grey light of a misty morning. Jared would find working in England again much different from working in Australia, she reflected unwillingly, warming her cold hands over the flames. Should he decide to stay, of course, she added impatiently, aware that she was allowing thoughts of Jared to intrude once again. For heaven's sake, it was by no means certain that he would stay. In his position, she doubted she would even consider it. He had made a good life for himself at the other side of the world, that was obvious from things he had said over dinner the night before. She knew that—and so must Ben.

A knock at the door which led to her secretary's office provided a welcome distraction. 'Come in, Joan,' she called, turning from the fire with some relief, only to find Maurice Woodhouse entering the room.

Joan Hedley's office opened into the corridor that led from one end of the old building to the other; consequently, unless they used the outer door, all Robyn's visitors came that way. All the same, she had not been expecting to see Maurice Woodhouse at this hour of the morning, and his coming to her office usually meant trouble.

He had disapproved of her promotion to acting managing director ever since Ben had put her there, and although he must know as well as anyone that it was really Ben he should blame, he had always directed his resentment towards Robyn and no one else. Perhaps he thought she had persuaded Ben to make her his deputy, Robyn thought wryly. If only he knew. Nothing could be further from the truth.

'Good morning,' he said now, levering his rotund body through the door and approaching Robyn's desk with an air of satisfaction. 'Well? Where is he, then? Didn't he drive down with you? I'd have thought he'd be wanting to get his hand in as soon as possible.'

Comprehension dawned. 'Oh—you mean Jared,' Robyn declared, turning from the fire to take up her position behind the desk with a certain sense of triumph. 'He's not here, Mr Woodhouse. As far as I know, he's not even out of bed.'

'But he *is* coming?'

Maurice Woodhouse regarded her dourly, and Robyn thought how pleasant it would be to hand over dealing with Morley's chief accountant to someone else. He had always tried to intimidate her and, if he hadn't succeeded, it was due in part to the fact that she could meet him on eye-level terms. For once, her height was not a disadvantage, and she straightened her spine now and faced him squarely.

'I don't know,' she replied, in answer to his question. 'Probably not today, anyway.'

Maurice Woodhouse frowned. 'What's that supposed to mean?'

Robyn controlled her temper. 'What is what supposed to mean, Mr Woodhouse?'

'You know.' He sighed. 'When is he coming, then? Didn't he tell you?'

Robyn looked down at the pile of mail Mrs Hedley had left on her desk to give herself time to compose her answer. Then, adopting a polite smile, she said, 'I don't even know if he intends to come to the office—today, or ever,' she responded smoothly. 'Now, if you've no further business, Mr Woodhouse——'

'You mean there's some doubt about it?' The man was not to be sidestepped and Robyn's nails dug into the desk, where the leather inlay gave way to weathered mahogany.

'I mean that you know as much as I do, Mr Woodhouse,' she replied steadily. 'If you want to know what Jared intends to do, I suggest you ask him. You know the number. Give him a ring.'

Woodhouse scowled. 'Well, it's a bloody rum show to me,' he muttered, pushing his hands into the pockets of his jacket. The suit had seen better days, and there were shiny patches to show this was a habit of his. But for once Robyn had him at a disadvantage, and it wasn't altogether unenjoyable.

'Yes—well, we'll both be enlightened in the fullness of time,' she declared briskly. 'Until then, I suggest we function as usual. Was there a problem, or did you just come to welcome Jared home?'

Woodhouse sniffed. 'You know that combing machine's on the blink again, don't you?'

'The engineer is coming to fix it today,' Robyn averred, flicking through the pile of letters. 'Anything else?'

'You haven't forgotten the representative from Weatherill's is coming this afternoon?'

'No. I haven't forgotten.' Robyn could afford to be patient. It was so good to feel in charge for once. 'Is that all?'

Woodhouse gave a reluctant nod. 'Doubtless Mr Morley will be putting me in the picture later today,' he declared. 'He'll know what's going on. I'll speak to him.'

And the best of luck! thought Robyn childishly, pulling a face at his back as he went out the way he had come in. Miserable old devil! She doubted women's emancipation got any further than his front door.

Joan Hedley came in as the chief accountant went out, just in time to catch the tail-end of Robyn's grimace. 'I hope that isn't for me,' she remarked good-humouredly, coming into the office and closing the door, and Robyn collapsed into her chair with a disarming giggle.

'That man is impossible,' she exclaimed, shaking her head at the older woman. 'I think he thought Jared would step immediately into Stephen's shoes. He actually expected him to be here this morning. He can't wait to get me out of this office.'

'Ignore him,' advised Joan Hedley shrewdly, taking up a position across the desk from her employer. 'So— is Jared enthusiastic about working at Morley's? Or hasn't Ben broached that yet? I can imagine he'd want to pick his moment.'

Joan Hedley had been at Morley's almost as long as Ben himself, and her plump, gregarious presence had been a source of comfort to Robyn in her first traumatic days as Stephen's successor. She had come to rely on her for more than just her knowledge of the business, and because she had no one else to talk to, Mrs Hedley had been the recipient of many confidences.

Now, accepting that Joan would understand the ignominy of her position, Robyn sighed. 'He didn't know about Ben,' she admitted ruefully. 'Stephen can't have written to him, or if he did, the letter never connected. In any event, he came home expecting to stay only a few days, and I had to tell him that Ben was disabled.'

'Dear me!' Joan was surprised. 'That must have been quite a shock for him. Had there been some mix-up over the mail?'

'I don't know.'

Robyn bent her head. In all honesty, she couldn't decide whether Ben had ordered Stephen not to inform his younger son, or whether Stephen himself had decided to keep the news from his brother. Obviously, if Stephen had done that, it would explain Ben's increasing bitterness towards Jared since his illness. Certainly, since Stephen's death, his attitude towards his younger son had changed, but that could have been caused by the circumstances of Stephen's death, and a desire for forgiveness before it was too late.

Whatever, at dinner the previous evening, Robyn had been unable to gauge what might have passed between the two men during the late afternoon hours they had spent closeted together in Ben's study. The truth was, she had been more concerned with ensuring that Daniel did not make too many demands on his uncle, although that excuse for keeping her son and her brother-in-law apart was as transparent as her excuses for not wanting to go to the airport had been.

Their arrival at the house had passed without incident. Saddlebridge had looked quite beautiful in the dying rays of a watery sun, the tall pines that formed a backdrop on the low hills behind giving its time-worn walls an air of stability. Robyn had always loved the house, even when she was a child and a visitor at Saddlebridge only at Stephen's father's invitation. The vicarage, where she had been brought up and where she had lived until her parents' deaths when she was eighteen, stood only a few hundred yards away, across the fields, and from her bedroom window she used to look at Saddlebridge and promise herself that she would have a house like that one day.

Of course, in those days she had never considered that marriage to Stephen would grant her wish. On the contrary, until Stephen was twenty-two and home from university, she had had more in common with Jared. But Stephen's return had changed many things, and she had been flattered to find herself the object of his attentions...

But that was all in the past and, observing Jared's reactions to his old home, she had realised that, in spite of his long absence, he still had some affection for the place. Indeed, as he entered the square hall, with its angled staircase and the gallery above, she had sensed his emotion, and only Mrs McCloud's intervention had prevented her from saying something she would probably have regretted afterwards.

Ben's emotion when he saw his son again was genuine enough. Whatever differences they had had in the past had been diluted by time and distance, and Jared's concern at finding his father in a wheelchair was too sincere to be faked.

The two men had retired to Ben's study before Daniel got home from school, and his disappointment at not being able to greet the uncle he had boasted about to his friends had made Robyn glad that Ben's study was sacrosanct.

'You'll see him later,' she had told the little boy firmly, picking up the satchel he had dropped on the hall floor and leading him into the kitchen. 'Come on. Mrs McCloud's made some ginger biscuits for you. I promise I'll let you meet him before you go to bed.'

Robyn had thought she was being extremely reasonable, in the circumstances, but she had not accounted for her son's curiosity. In spite of the fact that it was Monday, and the day *Blue Peter* was on children's television, Daniel had been hanging about in the hall when Jared had emerged from his father's study, and consequently Robyn had missed the first words they had said to one another. By the time she'd discovered what was happening, they were in Daniel's bedroom, sprawled out on the carpet, assembling the complicated track of his motor-racing kit.

It had been difficult to decide what Jared had been thinking at that moment. When she had appeared in the doorway, her face flushed with vexation, mouthing silly phrases about Daniel making a nuisance of himself and her not knowing where he was, Jared had got immediately to his feet and apologised for monopolising the boy. 'I didn't realise you might be worried,' he'd said. 'Dan and I have just been getting to know one another.'

'Don't call him Dan!'

Her reaction to his abbreviation of the boy's name had revealed how uptight she was, and Jared had made some excuse about changing for dinner and left them. Left her with Daniel's indignation, too, she remembered. And provided her son with the perfect excuse to appeal to his grandfather to be allowed to stay up for dinner. In the normal way, Daniel was in bed before Robyn and Ben had their evening meal, but for once Ben had been sympathetic.

'Why not let him stay up, Robyn?' he'd suggested, even though he usually didn't like the boy seeing that he had to have his food cut up for him. 'It is a special occasion, after all.' And what could Robyn have said which would not have sounded ungracious at the least?

'So how did they get on?' Joan was asking now, and Robyn dragged her thoughts back to the present with a distinct effort.

'You mean—Jared and Ben?' she murmured softly, and Joan shrugged.

'Who else?' she asked, and Robyn forced a smile.

'Um—fairly well, I think,' she replied, making an effort not to think about her son and Jared. 'In any event, they're still talking to one another, which is something. When—when Jared was younger, their conversations were more like confrontations.'

'I know.' Joan laughed. 'They've had a few of those in this office over the years. I used to think it was because they were so different, but now I'm sure it was because they are so much alike.'

'Alike!' Robyn sounded sceptical. 'I wouldn't have said Jared was like his father. Stephen, perhaps.'

'Oh, Stephen looked like him, I grant you that,' said Joan consideringly. 'And in some ways Stephen was like his father, too. They neither of them—well, made very good husbands, did they?'

Robyn bent her head. 'You could say that.'

'Oh, I know what I'm saying, all right,' said Joan wryly. 'And, as far as Stephen was concerned—well, I think you know, I'm not trying to hurt you. But Ben—he had two bites of the cherry, so to speak, and both times he ended up in the divorce court. Not that he wasn't well rid of Stephen's mother. She was a right bitch at times, and I think they deserved each other. But Jared's mother, she was different, and I think Ben resented the boy because he reminded him of what happened.'

Robyn looked up. 'What did happen? I don't think I understand.'

Joan frowned. 'You mean, no one ever told you?'

'Told me what?'

'That the night Jared was born, Ben was in Leeds with another woman.'

'No!'

'Oh, yes.' Joan grimaced. 'It's old history now, but Eve—that was the second Mrs Morley's name, of course—well, she went into premature labour, and had to be rushed into Sheffield General. For a while, it was touch and go whether either she or the baby would survive. They were desperate to find Ben, to tell him, to get him to the hospital to be with her, but no one knew where he was. At least, that was what they said at first. Later on, one of his pals got worried and spilled the beans, and that was how they found him.'

Robyn's lips parted. 'I never knew.'

'Why should you? You were only a kid at the time. Anyway, that was the beginning of the end so far as Eve was concerned. She stuck it out for a few more months, and then she walked out on him, too.'

'Leaving her son behind,' said Robyn. 'Oh, I could never do something like that.'

'Well, Jared was Ben's son, too,' said Joan wryly. 'And she knew he could do more for him than she could. I don't think she ever realised that Ben would blame Jared. I think he did love her, you see. Even if he had a funny way of showing it. He was really cut up when she died.'

'I see.' Robyn shivered. At least she had been spared that particular humiliation. And Daniel need never know the kind of man his father had been.

'Anyway, we'll see what happens now,' remarked Joan lightly, as Robyn turned back to the letters. 'Jared always did have a conscience, which is probably just as well. He may have come home intending not to stay but, unless he's changed completely, I don't think he'll be going back.'

Robyn tilted her head. 'He's six years older, Joan. He's twenty-seven now. Not a boy any more.'

Joan regarded her shrewdly. 'So you do think he's changed.'

'I didn't say that.' Robyn was evasive.

'What are you saying, then?'

'Oh——' Robyn picked up a biro and chewed the end uneasily '—I just think we should—reserve judgement.

He seems to have a very satisfactory life out in Sydney. Why should he give all that up just to please his father?'

'His *sick* father,' inserted Joan irrepressibly, making for the door. 'I'm going to make some coffee. Do you want a cup?'

All day, Robyn waited for Jared to put in an appearance, but at five o'clock, when she went out to get into her car, he had still not turned up. Folding her long legs behind the wheel, Robyn slammed her door rather more forcefully than usual, aware as she did so that she was endeavouring to expunge some of the frustration that had built up over the day. Perhaps because of Maurice Woodhouse's certainty that Jared would come in, she had convinced herself he would, too, and the fact that he hadn't had become increasingly suspect.

Where was he? she wondered. And where was Daniel? The possibility that they might be together was always foremost in her mind, and it was this, as much as anything, which had caused her to leave the office a full half-hour earlier than usual. In fact, lately she had still been working long after the rest of the staff had gone home, and because of the day she had taken off to go to the airport to meet Jared, she could have done with the extra time. But Daniel—and her peace of mind—had proved more important than the latest batch of production figures, and she had brought the file of papers with her to work on at home.

She could see the lights of Saddlebridge long before she turned on to the private road that led to the house. It stood in a wooded valley, just outside of the village of Saddleford, and the road winding down into the valley over Saddleford Tor gave a bird's-eye view of its many chimneys. It was some twenty minutes drive from the mill at Ebbersley on a good day, and perhaps fifteen minutes longer if the roads were icy. Saddleford Tor had been known to claim its own share of victims in the bad weather, but Robyn had driven that way so many times she was sure she could have done it blindfold.

However, this evening, all she had to contend with was the slow-moving stream of vehicles held up by a heavily laden tractor, which shouldn't have been out on the road after dark, anyway. Patience, Robyn, she schooled herself, as the cavalcade descended towards the village at a frustrating fifteen miles an hour, but her fingers were gripping the wheel with unwarranted force by the time she reached the turn-off for home.

Light was spilling from several windows as she brought the estate car to a halt on the tarmacked forecourt before the house. The mellow illumination from half a dozen uncurtained windows acted like floodlights on the drive, and Robyn allowed the familiarity of the scene to soothe her ruffled nerves. She was behaving foolishly, she chided herself, collecting her bag and briefcase from the back of the car. Rushing home, because she was afraid of what Jared might say to her son. What could he say, after all? Daniel was only a child, a baby; too young to be involved in affairs which had occurred long before he was even born. Just because she had once, very briefly, done something she had lived to regret, was no reason to assume Jared might use that knowledge to turn her son against her. Jared wasn't like that. He was not vindictive. If he had intended to cause trouble, he could have done so years ago. But he hadn't. He had gone away. And his reasons for coming back now were nothing to do with her.

All the same, as she walked into the house, the presentiment that all was not as it should be swept over her again. Everything looked the same. There were flowers in the silver bowl that stood on a rectangular table below the curve of the stairs, spilling their reflected colour in a waterfall of autumn shades. The lights were on in the gallery above, and the soft illumination gave warmth to the family portraits that mounted along the stairs. There was the smell of home baking emanating from the area of the kitchen, and Mrs McCloud herself to greet her as she took off her jacket to hang it away.

But, although she endeavoured to dispel her unease, it persisted in invading her stomach. Where was Daniel? she wondered. Why hadn't he come running to meet her, as he usually did? And where was Jared? What had he been doing all day?

'You're early, Robyn,' said Mrs McCloud pleasantly, taking her jacket from her, and draping it over her arm. 'You're looking tired. Did you not have a good day?'

For tired read old, thought Robyn tensely, running a nervous hand down the seam of her skirt. 'Just average,' she replied, glancing about her with assumed nonchalance. 'Er—where's Daniel? He's usually the first to hear the car.'

'Och, he's not here,' said Janet McCloud comfortably, turning to hang Robyn's jacket in the closet, and thus missing the revealing look of dismay that crossed her mistress's face at her words. 'Jared's taken him down to the village. Your father-in-law decided he wanted lamb chops for dinner this evening, and I didn't have a spoonful of mint jelly in the house.'

'I see'

Robyn had managed to control her features by the time Janet turned from the closet, but her response must have sounded clipped, because the housekeeper gave her a rueful smile. 'He didn't expect you'd be back so early,' she said. 'But they won't be long, and in the meantime, why don't I make you and Mr Morley a nice cup of tea.'

Tea! Robyn caught her breath. Yes, perhaps that would be a good idea. If she put several spoonfuls of sugar into it, maybe it would relieve the shock she had just suffered.

Nodding now, she summoned a tight smile. 'Why not?' she said. 'Where is Mr Morley? I expect he's waiting for a run-down on the mistakes I've made today.'

Janet laughed. 'He's in the library. He had me light the fire in there earlier today. You know, he really seems to have taken new heart since he learned Jared was coming home.'

There was nothing Robyn could say to that, and the two women parted company—Mrs McCloud to prepare a tray of afternoon tea, and Robyn to go in search of her father-in-law and regale him with the day's events. What Robyn would have really liked to do was seek the sanctuary of her room, in an effort to come to terms with the fact that Jared was Daniel's uncle, that it was natural that her son should find his father's brother an exciting person to talk to, and that, having so recently lost his father, he should want to be with him. But, of course, she couldn't—not least because she wanted to be there when they got home. She wanted to see for herself how Jared and Daniel reacted to one another, and to gauge from Daniel's expression if any damage had been done.

The library at Saddlebridge overlooked the gardens at the back of the house, although at this time on a winter's evening the long velvet curtains were drawn against the chilly landscape outside. A large, comfortable room, it served as both library and living-room, Robyn sharing Ben's assertion that it was less draughty than the sitting-room. Many of the ground-floor rooms at Saddlebridge were only used in summer now, when it wasn't necessary to heat them to a living temperature. Since Ben's illness, and its consequent curtailment of much entertaining, the family confined themselves to the library and the sitting-room, using the morning-room to eat in instead of the lofty dining-hall. Of course, there was Ben's study, too, and his private apartments, where he could go to get a little peace and quiet. Daniel could be quite demanding on occasion, but even he knew better than to invade his grandfather's private domain.

Now Robyn opened the library door, and put her head round it. 'Am I intruding?'

Ben Morley was seated in his wheelchair beside the wide fireplace, gazing into the flames cast by a handful of logs burning in the grate. He wasn't doing anything, just watching the flames, his hands folded together over the rug that warmed his knees. One side of his face was slightly distorted, the paralysis which had followed the stroke leaving the muscles on the left side of his body to droop and atrophy. But that side of his face was turned away from her, and his smile was warm as he greeted her and bade her to come in.

'Sit down,' he said, and although his speech was distorted, too, Robyn had no difficulty in understanding him. 'Jared and Daniel have gone down to the village. But I don't expect they'll be long.'

'No. Mrs McCloud told me,' said Robyn, taking the armchair opposite. 'Goodness, it's warm in here. Have you got the radiators on, as well?'

'Jared was cold,' said Ben defensively, and then, seeing the faintly sceptical gleam in her eyes, he grimaced. 'Well, *I* was cold, then. It's been a cold day. It could freeze tonight.'

'It could,' agreed Robyn drily, and said no more about the temperature in the room. Instead, she loosened the collar of her shirt and ran her cold fingers into the opening. 'So—how are you?'

'I'm all right.' Ben was always offhand about his health. 'How are you? Did Merrick come?'

Merrick was the representative from Weatherill's, the company Maurice Woodhouse had mentioned earlier in the day. 'Yes, he came,' she said, easing her shoulders back against the squashy leather upholstery. 'He said it's going to cost us rather more to replace the conveyor belt than we had expected.'

'Oh, well...' Ben was philosophical. 'It has to be done. It's been breaking down far too frequently lately. We're getting behind on orders. And now that Jared's here...'

Robyn bent her head. 'Have you talked to him?'

'Who? Jared?'

'Who else?'

'Of course I've talked to him.' Ben was impatient now. 'What do you think? That we just sit staring at one another?'

Robyn sighed and lifted her head. 'That's not what I meant, and you know it.'

The right side of Ben's mouth twisted. 'You mean—about him staying,' he said, and it wasn't a question.

'I mean about him staying,' agreed Robyn tensely, wondering what she would do if Jared agreed to do as his father wished. She had intended to stay at Saddlebridge, whatever happened, for Daniel's sake. But that was before she had seen Jared again, before she had realised the past was never dead.

'Well, of course he's going to stay,' Ben declared fiercely. 'He's my son, isn't he?'

Robyn held herself stiffly. 'You've actually asked him?'

Ben muttered something not very complimentary under his breath. 'I don't have to ask him,' he admitted, after a moment. 'Now, where the devil is he? I want some tea.'

'Janet's bringing some,' said Robyn, unconsciously relaxing again. To reinforce her words, there was a tap at the door at that moment, heralding the arrival of the housekeeper with a loaded trolley.

'Dear me, you cannot breathe in here,' she exclaimed, as she set the trolley by Robyn's chair. 'Would you not like me to put a guard around that fire, Mr Morley? We don't want you catching fire, now do we?'

Ben gave her a sarcastic look. 'There's no danger of that,' he assured her grimly. 'But pour me some tea, Robyn. I can always use it to damp myself down.'

Janet's good-humoured features took on a reproving expression. 'Just because Jared's come home, and you're feeling full of yourself, don't go overdoing it. We'll have to pick up the pieces after he's gone, just you remember that.'

'He won't *be* going,' said Ben irritably, his good hand kneading the arm of his chair, but, before either Janet or Robyn could make any reply, there was the sound of running footsteps across the hall and presently Daniel appeared in the open doorway, flushed and beaming and gasping for breath.

The sight of her son had always given Robyn a feeling of joy. Tall for his age, with silky dark hair and a faintly olive complexion, he was a good-looking boy, with none of the tubby stockiness of some of his schoolmates. He wore the grey trousers and green and grey striped blazer of the small preparatory school he attended with an easy indolence, reminiscent of his father, but for once Robyn could not rise to greet him with her usual surge of pride. Instead, she knew a sense of indignation that he should not have been here when she got home, and a bitter condemnation at his evident state of excitement.

'Mum?' he said, a little less confidently, reacting to her grim expression. 'You're home early.'

'And you're late,' said Robyn coldly, hearing the repression in her voice, but unable to do anything about it. 'And how many times have I told you not to run about the house? Your shoes scrape the floor, and Mrs McCloud has just spent half the day polishing it.'

'Hardly that,' said another voice, as the tall lean frame of her brother-in-law appeared behind her son. One hand came to rest on Daniel's thin shoulder, and because she refused to lift her eyes to his face, she saw the way his strong fingers squeezed the flesh reassuringly. 'Not unless she wants us to break a leg,' Jared appended drily. 'Isn't that right, Janet?'

'Och, I dare say you're right; about the polishing, anyway. But,' she glanced awkwardly at Robyn's taut features, 'the little one oughtn't to run about the house. It's not—proper.'

'It's not important,' Jared corrected her crisply, pushing the boy before him into the room. 'Dan, go and tell your grandfather where we've been,' he added in an undertone. 'I want to have a private word with your mother.'

'I wish you would call him Daniel,' hissed Robyn tensely, busying herself with pouring Ben's tea. She had no intention of having any private words with Jared. Not until she had had time to control the emotions she had felt on seeing them together.

'Now—or later. It's up to you,' said Jared, taking no notice of her muttered reproof, and it took all Robyn's self-control to remain seated when what she would really have liked to do was leave the room.

'Tea, Ben?' she said instead, aware of her son's troubled stare as he took up a position beside his grandfather's chair. 'Er—would you like a sandwich? Or would you rather settle for one of Janet's famous scones?'

'Just the tea,' said the older man frowning, evidently aware of the sudden atmosphere in the room. 'Um—two spoons of sugar. That's right. Thank you, that's all I need.'

'Can I have a biscuit, please?' asked Daniel, watching his mother doubtfully, and although she wanted to re-assure her son, too, Robyn heard herself caution him once again.

'It's *may* I have a biscuit, please,' she corrected him bleakly. 'And no, you may not. You'll be having your supper in less than an hour.'

Daniel's mouth quivered, but for once he didn't argue with her. Instead, he flung himself down on the floor in front of the fire and regarded her reproachfully with un-comprehending green eyes.

'Where have you been?' Ben asked, in the vacuum that followed this latest exchange, and Daniel struggled to regain his confidence.

'We went to Bakewell,' he told his grandfather rather timidly. And then, aware that he had his mother's at-tention as well, he scrambled into a cross-legged pos-ition and added with more confidence, 'They didn't have any mint jelly in Saddleford, you see, and Uncle Jared said we might as well try somewhere else. That's why we've been so long. We went over the moor road, and when we came back Uncle Jared let me steer the car all the way down into the village.'

'Did he?' Ben's response was only mildly reproving, but Robyn knew an almost uncontrollable desire to scream. What a crazy, reckless thing to do! To let a boy of *seven* steer a powerful car like the Rolls-Royce. It was ridiculous, madness! Just the sort of thing Jared would do, to show her how easily her son could be corrupted.

She couldn't take any more. Putting her half-empty cup of tea aside, she got abruptly to her feet. 'If you'll excuse me,' she said, realising as she did so how ridiculously formal she sounded. 'I—er—I want to go over some papers before dinner.' She licked her dry lips. 'Daniel, I'll see you upstairs in fifteen minutes. If you're thirsty, ask Mrs McCloud to give you a glass of milk, and then start getting undressed if I'm not there.'

Daniel nodded. 'All right.'

'Good.' Robyn walked to the door. 'I'll see you—later,' she added, addressing her remark to no one in particular, and let herself out of the room without a backward glance.

She heard the library door open again as she went up the stairs, but she didn't stop to see who had emerged. Daniel or Jared; she had no wish to speak to either of them at that moment, and she gained the sanctuary of her own room with a heartfelt sigh of gratitude.

But her relief was short-lived. She had scarcely time to switch on the lamps and acknowledge the pink and gold appointments of the room, before someone knocked at the door behind her. She knew who it must be. Daniel was unlikely to push his luck a third time, and there was no earthly reason why Janet should have followed her upstairs. It had to be Jared, and she clasped her hands impotently, wishing she could just pretend not to hear.

Shivering slightly, she moved away from the door, but before she could compose herself to make any response the handle turned, and the door opened. As she swung round then, marshalling her defences, Jared came into the room, and her eyes widened indignantly at this display of downright arrogance.

'What do you think you're doing?' she exclaimed, as he closed the door behind him, and Jared's lips twisted at her transparent outrage.

'What do you think?' he countered, leaning back against the panels for a moment before advancing across the soft gold carpet. 'I told you I wanted to talk to you. I do. About my son!'

CHAPTER THREE

'*YOUR* son?'

Robyn felt as if every muscle in her body had frozen into immobility. Which was probably just as well, she reflected later. Without that traumatic stiffness, her legs might well have refused to support her. As it was, she could at least face Jared with a simulation of impassivity, even if inside herself she was a petrified mass of jelly.

'Yes, *my* son,' said Jared flatly, pausing directly in front of her and surveying her without emotion. 'You're not going to try and deny it, are you? We both know it's true, and it's a little late now to make an issue of it.'

Robyn swallowed. 'I don't know what you're talking about!' she exclaimed, totally incapable of responding in any other way. 'Of course Daniel's not your son. He's Stephen's. Stephen was his father. And just because he's dead is no reason to try and cast doubts on the relationship.'

Jared expelled his breath heavily. 'So that's the way you're going to play it,' he said, folding his arms across his chest. He was wearing a dark suit today, she noticed, the kind of suit he would wear to go in to the office, and she wondered if he had considered doing that and then had second thoughts. In any event, the dark grey mohair was an attractive foil to the sun-bronzed darkness of his skin, the bleached lightness of his hair bright against the formal collar of his jacket.

But she shouldn't be thinking such thoughts, she reminded herself unsteadily. What he was wearing, how he looked, whether or not she had once found him attractive, were not points at issue here. He didn't know— he couldn't know—anything about Daniel. He was simply baiting her, testing her, trying out a theory; anything to get her to say something to incriminate herself.

'I'm not sure what you mean by "playing",' she said, turning deliberately away to glance at her reflection in the leaved mirrors of the dressing-table. But what she saw did not please her. She looked a mess, she thought critically, seeing nothing to admire in her pale, strained features and angular body. Even her hair, which had once been rich and lustrous, seemed to have lost its shine, and she couldn't help the treacherous thought that he must see how she had aged.

'Will you look at me when you talk to me?' Jared snapped then, catching her arm and swinging her round to face him. His strong fingers ground the thin layer of flesh against the bone, and when she winced he released her abruptly. 'Get it into your head, Robyn,' he muttered, as she massaged the place where his fingers had been, 'I know. Do you understand me? I know Daniel's my son.' He swore softly as she continued to stare blankly at him. 'I've known for years, didn't you realise that? Ever since he was born, I guess. But there was nothing I could do about it then. Now there is.'

Robyn's frozen limbs were thawing, and she began to tremble. 'You don't know anything——'

'Don't I?' Jared's mouth was grim. 'How long were you married before Daniel was born? Eight months, wasn't it?'

Robyn's heart was pounding. 'He was an eight months' baby.'

'Was he?' Jared looked at her contemptuously. 'That's not what I heard.'

'What could you hear? You weren't even here when Daniel was born,' she protested swiftly. 'You were away at college. You didn't even come home for his christening.'

'No.' Jared inclined his head. 'And you know why.'

'I don't.' Robyn pressed the palms of her hands together. 'In any case, how do you know Stephen and I didn't—didn't——'

'Anticipate the happy day?' Jared suggested sardonically. 'You forget, Robyn, you weren't exactly—experienced, when I touched you.'

'Which makes it all the more despicable that you did!' she choked. 'How can you boast about a thing like that?'

'I'm not boasting.' Jared's jaw was grim. 'I'm just trying to get you to be honest, for once in your life.'

'And how honest were you? Seducing your brother's fiancée?' she demanded harshly. 'In any case, after that I had nothing to lose, did I?'

Jared's nostrils flared. 'I didn't seduce you.'

'You're saying it was my fault?' Robyn quivered uncontrollably. 'I suppose it might sound like that to an outsider. After all, I was older than you. I should have known better than to trust you——'

'For God's sake!' Jared cut in to this painful tirade. 'I'm not blaming anyone——'

'How could you?'

'—for Daniel's conception——'

'Daniel is *not* your son!'

'—I'm only trying to make you see it's no use pretending any more.'

'I'm not pretending.'

'You are,' Jared groaned. 'Robyn, for once in your life, be honest with me. Admit it. Admit that I'm Daniel's father. For pity's sake! Tell me the truth!'

'I am telling you the——'

Robyn broke off abruptly as the door opened behind him. Her fingers sprang to her lips, as if to stifle her words, and Jared turned slowly to confront the subject of their disagreement. Daniel, his expression mirroring his confusion at finding his uncle in his mother's bedroom, clung curiously to the handle, his eyes darting doubtfully from one to the other.

'Mum?' he said appealingly, and, realising this was her opportunity to escape any more questions, Robyn brushed past her inquisitor.

'I thought I told you to get undressed,' she exclaimed, detaching her son's fingers from the door and urging him outside, into the corridor beyond. Be thankful he didn't, she admonished herself silently. Without Daniel's intervention, goodness knew what Jared might have done.

'I heard voices,' said Daniel, looking at her anxiously, and Robyn's mouth suddenly felt unpleasantly dry.

'Voices?' she echoed faintly, and Daniel nodded.

'Were you and Uncle Jared arguing?' he asked innocently, revealing by his question that he had heard nothing incriminating. 'Don't you like Uncle Jared, Mum? Is that why you were cross because I was out when you got home?'

Robyn felt an unwelcome wave of colour invade her cheeks. 'Don't be silly, Daniel!' she exclaimed, hurrying him along the corridor towards his own room. 'I—of course I like Uncle Jared. It's just that—well, we were talking about something that happened a long time ago.'

'Before I was born?' asked Daniel persistently, and Robyn, aware that Jared had come out of the room behind them and was standing watching their hasty retreat along the corridor, nodded unwillingly.

'Um—long before you were born,' she agreed, propelling him into his own room. 'Now, come on. It's time for your bath. I'll go and turn on the taps, while you take off your clothes.'

It was comparatively easy to avoid Jared for the remainder of the day. Pleading a headache, she managed to excuse herself from the evening meal, consoling her conscience with the thought that Ben would probably appreciate the chance to have a private talk with his son. Instead, Robyn spent the evening going over the production figures she had brought from the office, finding some escape from her thoughts in the questions she still had to answer.

All was not well with Morley Textiles. She didn't like to worry Ben, but since Stephen's death she had discovered a number of discrepancies in the figures. She wasn't absolutely sure, but it looked suspiciously as if someone had been withdrawing capital from the company over a number of years. Since Ben's crippling illness, the amount of plant investment had dropped considerably and, in consequence, they badly needed an injection of funds. Morley's was a private company, with a limited number of shareholders, and any drain on capital assets was bound, sooner or later, to have an effect. She would gladly have discussed the figures with Maurice Woodhouse, if he had shown himself even half-way willing to accept her as Stephen's deputy. But he hadn't. Instead, she had been left with the unpleasant suspicion that perhaps he had something to hide for, failing that, the alternative was too unpalatable to consider. Despite his faults, she refused to believe that Stephen had been systematically defrauding the company in his father's absence. The idea was too ludicrous. Stephen wouldn't have done that. There had to be another solution.

Later, lying in bed, Robyn wondered why she was trying so hard to find an answer. It wasn't really her problem—not any more. Jared—or if not Jared, then someone else Ben appointed—was going to have to take charge of Morley Textiles. She had been simply a substitute, and an amateur one at best. She had more important problems to contend with. Particularly now.

She was too practical to believe that that one brief confrontation with Jared was all she was going to have to face. He hadn't finished with her yet. She had glimpsed the impotent fury in his face when Daniel had innocently interrupted them, and if he could have sent the boy away without arousing any suspicion, he would have done it. But he had known that alienating possibly his greatest ally would not be the most sensible thing to do, and in consequence she had got away with it. But that wouldn't always be the case, she knew that. She couldn't rely on Daniel to extricate her from every difficult situation. On the contrary, it was Daniel himself who was at risk here, and she mustn't give Jared the chance to use her son against her.

All the same, until tonight she had had no idea how precarious her position might be. To think she had been afraid that Jared might choose to resurrect a relationship that should never have been allowed to happen! She had actually flattered herself into believing he might still find her attractive, and she had steeled herself to repulse his advances. How naïve she still was. Jared had torn her foolish notions of romance down about her ears, and attacked the one area of her life she had thought inviolable. But Daniel was hers; he was her son; and no one, least of all the man who had violated her, should flaw that association.

And, if she stood firm, she had nothing to worry about, she told herself for the umpteenth time. There was nothing he could do, nothing he could prove. Daniel was Stephen's son; everybody believed that. Heavens, she had told herself so so many times, she almost believed it herself...

In spite of her troubled thoughts, Robyn fell asleep at last, and it wasn't until her alarm woke her that she stirred to reluctant consciousness. In the normal way, she had no difficulty in getting up in the morning, but the sense of something ominous hanging over her head made this morning slightly different. Robyn had a strong desire to bury her head in the pillow and hibernate until Christmas. Perhaps, by then, the problem of Jared would have resolved itself, she thought hopefully, although something told her that running away from her troubles was not likely to improve their character.

She was drying her hair in the bathroom when Janet McCloud appeared with a tray of morning tea. 'I wondered if you were up,' she said, when Robyn grabbed her robe and came to the bathroom door. 'It's nearly eight o'clock. Don't you want any breakfast?'

Robyn managed a smile. 'Not this morning, thanks. Um—is Daniel up?'

'Up and dressed, and having breakfast with his uncle,' said Janet, unaware that anything she had said should perturb her employer's daughter-in-law. 'Don't you fret. I checked that he washed behind both ears. You just take your time now. You're looking rather peaky.'

Peaky! Robyn had an hysterical desire to laugh. If only Janet knew, she thought unsteadily. How much more of this could her nerves take? What was Jared trying to do to her?

It was too much trouble to try and gather the newly washed tangle of her hair into a neat chignon. Instead, she threaded it into a single, chunky braid, securing it with a leather thong before snatching up the clothes she had worn the night before. The cream shirt and plain navy skirt would have to do for another day. Flat-heeled shoes completed her ensemble, and she was half-way down the stairs before she realised she had forgotten to put on any make-up.

'Damn!' she muttered frustratedly, halting at the first landing, and then shrank back against a portrait of an earlier Morley ancestor as the morning-room door below the angle of the stairs opened and Jared himself emerged. He wasn't alone. Daniel was at his heels. And, as Robyn steeled herself to go and interrupt them, the boy caught Jared's hand and looked up at him expectantly.

'Can we?' he exclaimed, and Robyn felt like an eaves-dropper, listening in on a private conversation.

'We'll see,' Jared responded tolerantly, ruffling the boy's hair before opening the closet door and pulling out a leather jacket. It was an old jacket that Ben had sometimes worn, and Robyn had forgotten who it had belonged to until now. But seeing it fit over Jared's broad shoulders, with evident familiarity, adding another layer of warmth to the elegant dark suit he had worn the day before, she remembered.

'I've never been to York before,' Daniel was saying now, watching his uncle with interest. 'Grandpa was always too busy before he was ill, and Mum isn't really interested in stuffy museums.'

Jared thrust his hands into the pockets of his jacket. 'And what about your father?' he enquired, causing Robyn to catch her breath instinctively.

'Oh, Dad always said he didn't have the time,' confided Daniel frankly. 'We didn't see a lot of Dad, actually. Mum used to say he had a lot to do, looking after the business when Grandpa couldn't, but I don't think it was just that.'

'Don't you?' Jared seemed to hesitate a moment, and then he said, 'Why not?'

Robyn gasped then. Had the man no scruples? she wondered incredulously. Pushing herself away from the wall, she started down the stairs to break up this unholy alliance, but before she could interrupt them, Daniel added artlessly, 'Well, one of the chaps at school said my Dad was going out with his mother and——'

'Daniel!'

Robyn's outraged use of her son's name halted him in full spate, and she had the doubtful satisfaction of seeing his face suffuse with colour.

'Oh—hello, Mum,' he mumbled, casting a guilty glance at Jared from beneath his thick dark lashes. 'I didn't know you were there. I was just seeing Uncle Jared off to work.'

Robyn transferred her gaze to her brother-in-law, the actual words her son had used to excuse himself registering less at that moment than her anger at Jared's underhanded means of getting information.

'Have you no shame?' she demanded, staring at Jared with scornful eyes. 'My God! I didn't think you'd sink as low as to pump Daniel about his father! Stephen's dead, for heaven's sake! At least have some respect for his memory!'

Daniel looked near to tears, and Jared's mouth thinned to a cruel line. 'You know I could argue that Stephen should have had more—respect for his—family,' he commented coldly. 'And we all create—complications when we—play games in our own—backyard.'

The pauses in his narrative were eloquent with the real message he was trying to convey, and Robyn flinched from the raw hatred gleaming in eyes, as cold as a mountain lake. It was a warning, plain and simple, and she knew it. But who was he threatening to tell? Daniel? Or his father?

Jared's hand, patting Daniel's shoulder, reassured the boy. 'Cheer up,' he said, and the smile he gave the child transformed his grim features. 'It's not the end of the world,' he added, turning towards the door. 'Don't let a little difference of opinion upset you. Your mother and I have never seen eye to eye.'

It was not until the outer door slammed behind him that Robyn recalled what her son had said earlier. Looking down into his troubled face, she exclaimed fiercely, 'Where did you say he was going? As I came down the stairs, you said something about him going out.'

Daniel moistened his lips. 'Uncle Jared?'

'Who else?' Robyn was in no mood to be patient.

'Why, he—he's gone to the mill,' admitted Daniel unhappily. 'Oh, Mum, why are you looking like that again? I thought you and Grandpa wanted Uncle Jared to take over at Morley's.'

Sitting in the estate car some fifteen minutes later, on her way to Ebbersley, Robyn realised she should have taken the time to talk to her son before leaving the house. But her automatic reaction had been to get to the mill as quickly as possible, if only to reassure herself that Jared was not spreading his lies there, and creating problems she hadn't even considered.

She should have talked to Daniel first, she fretted now, realising she had been hopelessly naïve in imagining she could keep Stephen's behaviour from her son. But she had known nothing about this incident at his prep school, and the idea that Julia Forrester's son had actually bragged about his mother's affair with her husband was quite incredible. Did the woman have no shame? Of course, Julia was a widow, and perhaps she had considered she had nothing to lose in making their relation-ship public knowledge. But Stephen should have had more sense. Had he always been so indiscreet? Had she, Robyn, just been too trusting to notice what was going on?

Rubbing the tip of her nose with her knuckle, Robyn remembered clearly how shocked she had been the first time she found Stephen out in a lie. But, of course, she had been pregnant with Daniel at the time, and so full of her own guilt herself, she had foolishly done nothing about it.

And that had been the beginning of the end for their marriage, she admitted. Old habits die hard, and even clichés have a grounding in the truth. And, in all honesty, she had not been able to put all the blame on his shoulders. She had betrayed him before their marriage, nothing could alter that, and she had never found any pleasure in sex since. Oh, she had tried; God, how she had tried! She had even gone to see a marriage guidance counsellor, in the hope that someone else might be able to help her. But, in spite of her participation, nothing had worked. She had had to accept the unpalatable fact that it was as much her fault as his.

At least, that was what she had thought up until now. But when it came to Daniel, she was forced to draw the line, and the idea that her son believed his father was a womaniser caught at her emotions with a painful intensity.

And why had Daniel told Jared? she asked herself frustratedly. Why had he never confided in her? Why tell someone who was little more than a virtual stranger to him, when the person who loved him most in the world could have consoled his confused little heart?

She shook her head, forced to concentrate on the twisting curves of Saddleford Tor. The traffic this morning was thick and heavy, and the mist from the moors eddied across the road in wraithlike swirls. November, she thought wearily, why had Jared come home in November? Why couldn't it have been summer, with so many more opportunities for escape?

But Jared hadn't chosen his time, she reminded herself severely. He was here because Stephen was dead, and Ben had sent for him. She couldn't blame Jared for coming. She could only blame herself for handling it so badly.

She had expected to see Ben's Rolls-Royce occupying the space allotted to the managing director, but when she drove into the mill yard there was no sign of that elegant vehicle. The only car she didn't immediately recognise was a black Volkswagen Golf, with year-old number-plates, parked without ceremony beneath the office steps.

Now what? she wondered, deciding Jared had had second thoughts about coming to the mill after all. Could the car belong to the engineer from Weatherill's? Had the week's estimate they had given her been shortened overnight?

Locking the car, she slung her tweed jacket about her shoulders and headed for the steps. She would soon know. There were lights on in her office, which meant Joan Hedley was around. At least the secretary could be relied upon to handle any visitors in her absence. With her knowledge of Morley's, she could have run the place herself.

Perhaps she should talk to Joan about the accounts, Robyn reflected, as she climbed the steps. Sooner or later, someone was going to have to mention them, and perhaps it would be more sensible to get that particular problem out of the way before Jared became involved. It was silly to want to protect Stephen after the circumstances of his death, but she had to maintain the fiction, if only for Daniel's sake.

She had her arms full, with her handbag and her briefcase, and the additional effort of trying to keep her jacket about her shoulders, so she used her elbow to press down upon the handle of the door. She was concentrating so much on negotiating this obstacle that, when the door opened inward, she almost lost her balance, and it was left to the man inside to save her from a fall.

Strong hands prevented her from sprawling on the rug and, although her briefcase tumbled from her grasp, she was able to secure her footing. All the same, her jacket slipped off her shoulders so that the lean brown fingers encountered only silk-covered flesh, and her skin prickled alarmingly beneath each separate pressure.

He released her almost at once, but not before Robyn had experienced a most unwelcome reaction to his touch. During her embarrassing display of clumsiness, she had been made unavoidably aware of the warm male scent of his body, and when her breasts brushed the rougher texture of his jacket, she felt an unfamiliar tightening in her stomach. A sense of heat spread from there, down the quivering muscles of her thighs, and although she put it down to simple nervousness she couldn't deny the panic deep inside her. Once again, she wanted to turn and run, but she doubted if she had the energy.

'Are you all right, Robyn?'

As Jared bent to pick up her jacket and then close the door behind her, Robyn saw with some relief that they were not alone. Joan Hedley was standing by the desk with the mail; it was she who had spoken, and as Robyn took a cautious step forward, she quickly came towards her.

'I—er—I'm fine,' Robyn assured her hurriedly, casting a backward glance over her shoulder, and then switching her gaze back to Joan before Jared could meet her gaze.

'You nearly measured your length,' chided Joan, picking up her briefcase, and setting it on the desk. 'Come along. Sit down. You look as if you need something warm inside you.'

'Oh, no—really,' murmured Robyn anxiously, loath that Joan should leave them right at this minute. Once she'd got her breath back, once she'd controlled whatever impulse had aroused those feelings inside her, she would be OK. But, just at this moment, she needed Joan's support.

'Nonsense.' Joan was determined to be sympathetic. 'How about you, Jared? Would you like a nice cup of coffee? I know, let's all have a cup, shall we? Then you can tell us all about what you've been doing in Australia.'

'Why not?' Jared essayed evenly, and Robyn wondered if Joan had deliberately seated her at this side of the desk so that Jared could take his father's place. 'That sounds good,' he added, taking up the position that was vacant. 'Sugar, but no cream in mine, please, Joan. I guess you know how Mrs Morley likes hers.'

'Just about,' agreed Joan wryly, going out of the door, and as it closed behind her Jared sank into his father's chair.

There followed one of the most pregnant silences Robyn had ever had to endure. Seated in the visitor's chair, at right angles to the desk, she was intensely aware of Jared's gaze boring into her profile. What was he thinking? she wondered, pressing her damp palms down upon quivering knees. And why the devil didn't he say something—*anything*—instead of simply staring at her, subjecting her to this nerve-wracking appraisal?

'I—I suppose I should thank you,' she ventured at last, when the awful cessation of sound in the room was beginning to deafen her. If it was his intention to humiliate her, she had to thwart it, and allowing him to make the rules was not going to accomplish anything. She must not make the same mistakes with him that she had made with Stephen. Start as you mean to go on, she told herself fiercely, disliking having to resort to another cliché. But if once she let Jared get the upper hand, her position at Saddlebridge would become intolerable.

'Not if you don't want to,' he answered now, settling back in his chair and surveying her beneath lowered lids. 'Perhaps I should ask you if you really are all right. As Joan pointed out, you do look a bit—drained.'

Robyn turned her head. 'Don't you mean *old*?' she enquired stiffly, tilting her chin. 'You were never one to mince your words, Jared. What you mean is, I look my age. Don't worry. You won't offend me by speaking the truth.'

Jared pressed his hands down on the rim of the desk and came upright. 'That wasn't what I said—or what I meant.'

Robyn forced herself to meet his gaze. 'No?'

'No.' Jared's lips twisted. 'I didn't realise you wanted compliments from me, Robyn. My initial impression was that you still hated my guts.'

Robyn withdrew her gaze abruptly. It was difficult to make any response to that shocking pronouncement, and for several seconds she stared at her hands, clenching over her knees.

Then, realising she could not allow Joan to come back with the situation in its present state of impasse, she said huskily, 'I don't hate you, Jared. Why should I? I just— resent your treating me like a fool, and turning my son against me.'

Jared sucked in his breath. 'You're crazy! I'm not turning Dan against you. You're making a pretty good job of that for yourself.'

'Me?'

Robyn was forced to look at him then but, as if growing tired of the argument, Jared shook his head. 'Let's leave it for now, shall we?' he suggested flatly. 'I didn't come to the office to get embroiled in personal affairs. So long as you're OK, that's all that matters. I guess we've both changed in lots of different ways.'

Robyn expelled her breath unevenly. 'All right.'

'Good.' Jared seemed content with her answer. 'So— let's talk about something else, shall we? Bring me up to date with what's been happening. I'd like to know a little about our position before old man Woodhouse starts breathing down my neck.'

CHAPTER FOUR

In spite of its inauspicious beginning, the rest of the day was not half as bad as Robyn had anticipated. To be honest, she had to admit that most of its success was due to Jared's willingness to deal with her on a purely impersonal level, and, aside from a few interruptions, they covered a great deal of ground.

There were times during the day when Robyn was tempted to ask Jared what he intended to do about the business, when she knew an almost overpowering impulse to find out exactly what his future intentions were. But asking questions of that nature was too partial in the present situation, and, although she argued that she, of all people, had a right to know where she stood, she decided it was up to Ben to put her in the picture.

Joan eased the situation, of course, bustling in and out of the office, asking questions about Jared's life in Australia, and teasing him about the girls he had known there. She seemed to notice nothing amiss in the fact that the younger woman did not join in their careless bantering, and Robyn found it easiest to close her ears at these times. It was natural, she told herself, that she should feel some sense of distaste at Jared's laughing revelations. After all, too many things had happened for her to ever feel at ease with him again. The best they could achieve was a working relationship, with the possibility of renewed hostilities breaking out at any time.

At lunch time, she joined Joan Hedley in the staff canteen as usual. She had intended to skip the meal—she was never very hungry at lunch time, anyway—if Jared had been disposed to join them. But, just before twelve, he announced he intended to have a drink at the pub with Frank Beasley, so for an hour, at least, Robyn was able to relax and be herself.

'He hasn't changed much, has he?' Joan remarked, digging into steak and kidney pie with enthusiasm, and looking askance at Robyn's wilting cheese salad. 'I remember Ben bringing both boys to the office when they were still at school. Jared looked ever so sweet in his school uniform. If I'd had any kids, I don't think I could have sent them away to school like that.'

Robyn's lips twitched in spite of herself. 'Sweet?' she echoed. 'Jared looked *sweet*?'

'Yes.' Joan made a defensive face. 'He always was the nicest of the two. Oh—sorry, Robyn!' She sighed. 'Me and my big mouth! It's just that—well, I suppose I always had a soft spot for Jared, him being the youngest and all.'

'It doesn't matter.' Robyn managed to dismiss her apology. 'It wouldn't do for all of us to feel the same, would it? I suppose—I suppose my being older, more Stephen's age, if you like, I saw them differently.'

'Hmm.' Joan nodded. 'Although, you know, when you were younger, I used to think you were fond of Jared, too.'

'Fond?' Robyn struggled to control her colour. 'I—well, I suppose I was—very close to both of them. And when my parents died——'

'Oh, yes.' Joan shook her head. 'That was a tragedy, wasn't it? Ben certainly came to the rescue then, didn't he? I suppose you felt you had a lot to thank him for.'

'Yes, I did.' Robyn's tongue circled her upper lip. 'I had no relatives, you see. My mother and father were both only children, and when they were killed...'

'Ben picked up the pieces,' finished Joan gently. 'Of course. But then, he was only looking to the future, wasn't he? I mean, he always wanted you to marry Stephen, you know. I heard him say that, long before you two made it official.'

'Did he?'

Robyn couldn't remember that. As far as she was aware, Ben's suggestion that she should come and live at Saddlebridge had been entirely arbitrary. It had been five years after her parents' deaths that she had actually married Stephen. She could hardly believe that her father-in-law had been thinking of that when he offered her a home.

'Well, anyway, you did it, didn't you?' Joan pursued now, watching her intently. 'Married Stephen, I mean,' she added. 'Did—er—did you ever regret it?'

Robyn felt a deepening of colour below her cheek-bones. 'I suppose you think I should,' she conceded after a moment, and now Joan's plump features showed her discomfort.

'Not necessarily,' she murmured defensively. 'Oh, I'm just being an inquisitive old woman. Don't take any notice of me. I shouldn't have asked that question.'

'But you did.' Robyn toyed restlessly with the lettuce on her plate. 'I suppose that's what everybody's asking. Particularly now.'

Joan shrugged. 'Oh, I don't know——'

'Please.' Robyn was impatient. 'At least be honest with me, Joan. We both know how—and where—Stephen died. Carnthwaite bridge is on the way to Charnley. No one's been able to prove anything, but I doubt that he was alone when it happened.'

Joan stared at her. 'Do you think—*she*—left him there, without even calling the police?'

Robyn lifted her shoulders. 'Why else was he going in that direction?' She sighed. 'Oh, the police have been very tactful, due no doubt to Ben's influence, but I'm not a fool. The chances are that—that Stephen was dead and she was afraid of being implicated. It would have caused quite a scandal, wouldn't it? And all to no avail.'

'But he might still have been alive!' exclaimed Joan fiercely. 'If the ambulance had got there sooner——'

'No,' said Robyn flatly, interrupting her tirade, and Joan frowned.

'How do you——'

'His—his neck was broken,' said Robyn steadily. 'I imagine that's why the police didn't push the matter. There was no question of the time of death. Stephen died when the car plunged down the embankment.'

Joan shook her head. 'Oh, Robyn! I'm sorry.'

Robyn took a deep breath. 'Yes—well, it's all over now.'

'And you don't resent what happened?'

'Why should I?'

'Well...' Joan shifted uncomfortably. 'Now that Jared's come back... Oh, you know what I mean. Jared's probably going to take over the company. Don't you mind that Daniel's going to lose everything?'

'Ah...' Robyn acknowledged the proof of the gossip that was sweeping the mill. 'Well, that's no problem. Stephen may have had his faults, but he didn't neglect his financial responsibilities. Daniel and I are well provided for, and—and if Jared does decide to stay, we can easily make other arrangements.'

'Other arrangements?' Joan looked puzzled.

'Of course.' Although, until she voiced them, Robyn had hardly been aware that she had been thinking along these lines. 'Obviously, if Jared comes back to live at Saddlebridge, Daniel and I will leave. After all, he may decide to get married, and the new Mrs Morley wouldn't want us as unpaying tenants.'

Robyn left the mill before Jared, driving home through a veil of mist, thicker than the one that had coated the moors that morning. She had discovered that the black Golf was Jared's car, hired from the garage in Saddleford the night before. That was why he had had no need to use his father's Rolls. The powerful little hatchback was far easier to handle on the twisting moorland roads. It was strange; she would have expected him to hire a big Ford or a Rover. He could even have contacted one of the larger dealers in Sheffield and arranged for them to provide him with a Mercedes or a Volvo for the duration of his stay, but he hadn't. A psychiatrist would probably say he didn't need the support of phallic symbols, she reflected wryly. Unlike Stephen, who had driven a Jaguar for the past ten years.

Daniel was watching out for her when she got home. He looked over her shoulder expectantly as she came through the door, and she determinedly squashed her irritation at his obvious disappointment that Jared wasn't with her. Instead, she bent down and put her arms around him, giving him a warm hug; and, although he squirmed away from her, she could tell he was half relieved.

'Did you have a good day, darling?' she asked, straightening and unbuttoning her jacket. 'Have you been to see Grandpa? Is he feeling all right this evening?'

'Grandpa's fine,' said Daniel confidently, taking her jacket from her and hanging it away in the hall closet. He was proud of his recent ability to reach the hooks in the closet, and Robyn's nerves steadied at the familiar demands of home. 'And I came top in the arithmetic test we had this morning,' he added.

'Top!' Robyn was impressed. 'Did you tell Grandpa?'

'Yes.' Daniel closed the closet door and looked diffidently up at her. 'He said I must take after Uncle Jared. He said, at my age, Dad was no good at sums at all.'

Robyn felt as if a cold hand had invaded her stomach. 'Oh,' she said, her nerves responding to this new threat. 'Well, I shouldn't take too much notice of Grandpa. If your father hadn't been any good at sums, he could never have run Morley Textiles, could he?'

Daniel looked anxious. 'You're not still mad at me, are you, Mum?' he mumbled unhappily. 'I mean—because of what I told Uncle Jared.'

'Don't be silly!' The sharp words were out before she could prevent them, and Daniel stepped back a pace automatically. 'Oh——' Robyn sighed, and made a helpless gesture. 'Of course I'm not mad at you, Daniel. I just—don't think you should repeat schoolboy gossip to your Uncle Jared. He'll probably be returning to Australia in a few days, and I don't want you to get—hurt.'

'Grandpa says that Uncle Jared's going to stay here, and live with us,' argued Daniel swiftly, evidently as willing as she was to forget what he had heard about his father. 'He says that he only went to Australia because, so long as Daddy was alive, he had no interest in the company.'

Robyn could feel the muscles of her face tightening. 'Yes,' she said stiffly. 'Yes, well—your grandfather may be hoping——'

'No, he says Uncle Jared *is* going to stay,' Daniel interrupted her blandly, unaware that he was causing her distress. 'Isn't that great? He'll be able to use the room next to yours. There'll be four Morleys at Saddlebridge, just like there was before.'

'No!' Robyn almost choked on the word, and Daniel halted uncertainly.

'No?' He looked at her bewilderedly. 'But—why?'

'Why?' Robyn met her son's blank stare and chickened out. 'Um—well, your father hasn't even been dead two months!'

'Oh.' Daniel's face cleared. 'And you don't want Uncle Jared to sleep in Daddy's room. I never thought of that.'

'No. That's not what I——' Robyn broke off abruptly. 'Look,' she put a hand on his shoulder and propelled him towards the kitchen, 'you go and see what Mrs McCloud's got for your supper, hmm? I want to go and have a shower.'

'Aren't you going to see Grandpa first?' asked Daniel in surprise, and Robyn forced a thin smile.

'Not just at this moment,' she said, heading towards the stairs. 'You can tell Grandpa I'm home, and that I'll see you both in a little while.'

Closing the door of her room some few minutes later, Robyn leaned back weakly against the panels. At least she didn't have to worry this evening that Jared might come storming into her room and demand something from her she was not prepared to give. He was still at the mill, or at least he had been when she left; and if she knew Maurice Woodhouse, he would take the opportunity to confide his opinion of her efforts to the new managing director, if indeed Jared did intend to step into his brother's shoes.

The prospect made her feel unutterably weary and, stepping out of her shoes, she padded over to the bed. The temptation to take off all her clothes and crawl between the sheets was almost overwhelming and, perching on the edge of the mattress, she used both hands to resist the cowardly impulse.

She had to think, she told herself severely, lifting first one foot and then the other, surveying her toes, as if she might find the solution to her problems there. If what her son had said was true—and it was by no means certain that Jared was intending to return to Saddlebridge on a permanent basis—she and Daniel would have to find somewhere else to live.

The idea was daunting, to say the least. In spite of her desire to take herself and her son away from Jared's influence, she still had to consider where she was going to live. Did she intend to buy a house in Saddleford or Ebbersley, so that Daniel could continue at his present school and continue seeing his grandfather? Or was it her intention to move right away, and put this whole section of her past behind her?

She had no doubt how much easier it would be now if, when her parents had died, she had been left to fend for herself. If, at that time, she had had to find somewhere to live and a job of work to do, she might never have become involved with any of the Morleys. Their childhood friendship would have dwindled and been forgotten, and who knew, she might have married someone who could melt her frozen emotions.

But, instead, for the past fourteen years, she had been cushioned against the harsher realities of life. Ben had always treated her like the daughter he had never had, and only now was she realising how unreal her life had been.

She sighed and, getting up from the bed, she crossed the floor to her dressing-table. Sinking down on to the padded stool, she cupped her face with long, slender fingers, and studied her reflection. What had Jared *really* thought when he saw her? she wondered reluctantly. Probably that she neglected herself, she decided, smoothing a faint blemish in her cheek. When he had gone away, she had at least retained some confidence in her appearance, she acknowledged dully. But years of living with Stephen, of finding him out in a score of different ways, had taken their toll and, in spite of her insistence that she had been to blame, his continued pursuit of other women had become a burden.

It wasn't so much what he had been doing. She could live with that. Indeed, she was shamefully aware that she had welcomed the cessation in the demands Stephen had made upon her. When he had suggested moving his belongings into one of the spare rooms so that he wouldn't disturb her if he came home late, she had been only too happy to agree, and she had been grateful not to have to find excuses. But the constant gossip was what had hurt her most, invading her defences and under-mining her confidence. She had even stopped going into the village, because of the unspoken sympathy she could sense behind each friendly word, and if people thought she was stand-offish, it was a façade she had adopted.

Even so, over the years, she had learned to hide her feelings. Maybe that was why the almost six years between her and Jared's ages seemed to have stretched to ten and beyond. She probably looked old enough to be *his* mother, she thought, with rather less perspicacity. At any rate, he probably thought so, she reflected, even if he hadn't said it.

As she pressed her lips together in a sudden surge of indignation, Robyn's hands sought the leather thong that bound the chunky braid, and tore it free. Then, threading her fingers through the heavy mass, she pulled it loose about her shoulders, grimacing as its inky darkness gave her the sudden appearance of a witch. A witch with grey eyes, she assessed herself bitterly. They should have been green, like Daniel's—like Jared's.

By the time she had showered and changed into a one-piece black lounging suit, and secured her hair again in a more mature style, Robyn felt less threatened. Once again, she was allowing events to control her, she told herself severely. It was up to her to make her own decisions. She had nothing to fear if she kept her head. If she let Jared see she was running scared, then she deserved to be defeated.

All the same, walking into the library some fifteen minutes later took no small amount of courage. She didn't deceive herself that Jared's attitude at the mill would percolate into their personal relationship. He had come to England for a purpose, and she was only now beginning to suspect what that purpose might be. Whatever Ben said, Jared's motives were not wholly altruistic. But she could not tell his father what his real intentions were.

In the event, Ben was alone when she invaded his sanctuary, and his lined face showed his pleasure at her appearance. 'That's new, isn't it?' he asked, after she had asked after his welfare and received his usual disparaging reply. Looking down at the tapering legs of the trousers, Robyn had to acknowledge that she had not worn the suit before. 'It looks good,' her father-in-law continued, as she seated herself in the chair opposite and crossed her long legs. 'It's a change to see you wearing something youthful. Since Stephen died, you seem to have lost all interest in—well, in fashion.'

Since long before that, amended Robyn silently, only Ben hadn't noticed in those days. Or, if he had, he had never said anything. She wondered if Stephen's father still believed that she had been ignorant of his son's imperfections. She could hardly believe it, and yet Ben had always treated her with affection and respect. Perhaps that was his way of making up for what Stephen had done. Or perhaps he really thought she was that naïve! Oh, Ben, she thought unhappily, were we all deceiving each other?

'So what happened?' the old man asked now, and Robyn had to force herself to attend to what he was saying.

'What happened?' she echoed a little blankly. 'I'm afraid I——'

'Jared went to the mill, didn't he?' Ben's undistorted eye stared at her unblinkingly, and she expelled her breath.

'Oh—oh, yes,' she nodded, moistening her lips. 'Yes, he was there.'

'And?'

'And?' Robyn caught her lower lip between her teeth. 'Well, I think I've put him in the picture—as far as I can, of course. I believe Maurice Woodhouse wanted to have a word with him after I left.'

'And did he say anything to you?'

'To me?' Robyn looked at him uncomprehendingly. 'What about? He said a lot, of course. I don't think he's too keen on that timework scheme Stephen introduced, but you weren't very keen on——'

'About *staying*!' Ben interrupted her impatiently. 'Did he say anything to you about staying? Come on. You know what I'm talking about. Did he or didn't he?'

Robyn blinked. 'But I thought you said—at least, Daniel said——'

'Never mind what I said or what Daniel said. I want to know what Jared has said to you. He must have said something. You and he used to be so close!'

Robyn felt warm colour invade her cheeks. 'We were never *close*!'

'Nonsense! Of course you were. You were always the one Jared used to confide in.' He sighed. 'It's not as if I'm asking you to break a confidence or anything. I just want to know what his feelings are. Do you think he's prepared to stay? Has he given you any notion at all of what his plans might be?'

Robyn swallowed. 'But you said——'

'Look, I've told you. Forget what I said. That's not in question here. I want to know what the situation's like in Australia. Is there some woman there I should know about? What has Jared said to you?'

What indeed? thought Robyn painfully. If only she could discuss the things Jared had said with her father-in-law. But she couldn't. That aspect of their relationship could never be spoken of, and everything else was coloured by that knowledge.

'I don't honestly know what he thinks, or what he plans to do,' she replied at last. 'He—he seemed interested in what was happening, but you know him better than I do. Don't you know how he feels?'

'If I did, I wouldn't be asking you, would I?' muttered Ben dourly. 'Oh, I don't know, Robyn. I was sure when I sent for him that he'd jump at the chance to step into Stephen's shoes. Now I'm not convinced.'

Robyn expelled her breath a little unevenly. 'Oh,' she murmured. 'Um—why?'

Ben moved his shoulders in the semblance of a shrug. 'I don't know exactly. He's changed. Don't you find that? I've talked to him. He knows how I feel. But I'm damned if I can get a straight answer from him.'

Robyn bent her head. 'I see.'

'It's so damned galling,' the old man added bitterly. 'Who would have thought I'd have to go begging to him? He knows I'm vulnerable. He knows I can't *make* him do what I want. Do you think he's only humouring me by going to the office? Do you think he has any intention of moving back to England?'

Robyn shook her head. She didn't know how to answer him. For her own part, the idea that Jared might choose to return to Australia was a tantalising prospect. If he *did* refuse his claim to the mill and returned to Sydney, he was unlikely to come back, and the one fear she had had all these years would be removed. She and Daniel could stay at Saddlebridge, and the prospect of moving need never arise.

It was a selfish hope and she knew it, but she had lived too long with her fears for them to be put aside to appease an old man's whim. Besides, until Stephen's death, Ben had given little thought to his younger son. Could he really expect Jared not to see the hypocrisy behind his belated summons to the family home?

'I think—I think you'll have to wait and see,' Robyn said now, getting up from her chair and moving across to the tray of drinks sitting on the cabinet in the corner. She was suddenly in need of sustenance. 'Do you want a soda? Or are you going to wait until Janet brings your tea? She's late, isn't she? It's almost—heavens! *Six!*'

'Exactly.' Ben was offhand now. 'I had my tea almost an hour ago. Don't tell me this business over Jared is getting to you, too. Going straight upstairs when you get home. Not even asking how an old man was.'

Robyn sighed. 'I needed a shower, Ben. It's been a long day.' She paused. 'Now—do you want anything?'

'Yes. A stiff brandy and soda,' said Ben harshly, and Robyn gazed at him impatiently.

'You know the doctor said——'

'Yes, yes. I know what the doctor said,' Ben mimicked her irritably. 'But one alcoholic drink isn't going to kill me, more's the pity. Go on. Pour me one. Or do you want me to come over there and spill brandy all over the carpet?'

Robyn was reluctant, but she was quite aware that Ben was likely to do exactly as he said. And, considering how much he used to like his pre-dinner drink in the evenings, he had been extremely patient with the restrictions Dr Harrington had put upon him. With a feeling of helplessness, she measured a small amount of brandy into a balloon-shaped glass, and then added a good half of a bottle of soda to dissipate its potency.

She was handing the glass to Ben when the library door opened. Expecting it to be Daniel, she turned, with a smile on her face, to greet the newcomer. But it was not her son, it was Jared; and the sight of his tall, loose-limbed indolence, after the conversation she and his father had just been having, brought the embarrassing glow of colour back into her cheeks.

Jared frowned when he saw the glass in his father's hand, and brows, which were several shades darker than his hair, arched disapprovingly. 'Ought you to be drinking that?' he asked, addressing his question to his father, yet leaving Robyn in no doubt as to who he considered deserved the blame. But, before she could defend herself, Ben intervened.

'What do you care?' he demanded, fixing his son with an aggressive stare. 'What else is there for me to do, stuck here like a condemned prisoner? Not even sure the company I've worked and slaved for is going to pass on to my own flesh and blood!'

'Ah!'

Jared's expellation of breath was the only audible sound in the room after his pronouncement. Robyn took refuge in the gin and tonic she had poured herself, hardly daring to look at either man as the pregnant silence stretched. Oh, why had Ben had to make that statement while she was in the room? she asked herself wearily. She had known he was getting desperate, but it was less than three days since Jared had set foot in England. Couldn't he have waited? Couldn't he have played Jared's game a little longer? Who could tell? From Jared's point of view, the longer he stayed without making a decision, the more likely he was to remain. Saddlebridge was like that. It tended to wrap its coils about you and, after a while, you didn't want to leave.

She swallowed another mouthful of the gin, feeling its warmth spreading into her stomach, alleviating the chill that had suddenly gripped her. What was she thinking of? she thought frustratedly. Why should she care if Ben blew his only chance to persuade Jared to come back? *She* didn't want Jared to stay. If he stayed, she and Daniel would have to go, and that was something she didn't care to contemplate.

The action of Ben swallowing his brandy and soda in one gulp seemed to bring the uneasy silence to an end. Crossing the room to take the empty glass from his father's hand, Jared gave a faintly ironic smile.

'OK,' he said, straightening with the glass in his hand, surveying its pale dregs with a considering eye. 'OK. I'll stay.'

Robyn caught her breath, but the sound was drowned by Ben's sudden choking laugh. 'Do you mean it?' he exclaimed, grasping his son's wrist with his good hand and gazing up at him disbelievingly. 'My God! Do you mean it? Hell, Jared, I don't know what to say! Just that—well, I'm very happy. Very happy indeed.'

Jared's smile thinned. 'There is a condition.'

'A condition?'

Ben looked confused, and Robyn felt the paralysing grip of apprehension invade her limbs. Why was she so sure the condition had to do with her? she asked herself anxiously. It could be anything. It could even involve her departure from Saddlebridge as part of the deal. After all, Jared *wouldn't* want her here if he brought another woman into the house. There couldn't be two mistresses at Saddlebridge, and she couldn't believe there was not some woman in his life at the present time.

'Yes, a condition,' Jared was saying now, forcing her to pay attention to his words. 'As a matter of fact——' he turned his head and looked at her '—it has to do with Robyn.'

'Robyn?' Ben frowned. 'What about Robyn? This is her home, Jared. I thought that would be understood——'

'Oh, please!' Robyn broke in to his words, her quickened breathing giving a nervous tremor to her speech. 'I—well, that is—we—Daniel and me, I mean—naturally we can't stay here indefinitely——'

'If you'll both stop trying to anticipate me, I'll explain,' said Jared flatly, setting his father's empty glass on the tray and surveying the other two people in the room with a cool green gaze. 'As I said, it does have to do with Robyn, but not in the way either of you think. I suppose mainly it has to do with—Dan,' he added, and Robyn's heart took a sickening leap.

'Dan?' said Ben doubtfully. 'What about Dan?'

'Well...' Jared was evidently enjoying Robyn's consternation and was in no hurry to relieve it. 'We all know that if—if Stephen hadn't died, Dan would have eventually inherited the company.'

'Yes, yes.' Ben was impatient. 'So?'

'So, I propose I make Dan *my* heir. It makes sense, doesn't it? It's only fair,' he added, his green gaze vanquishing the instinctive defence Robyn strove to gather. 'Morley's should be his. I think we're all agreed on that. And it means Robyn and her son can stay on here at Saddlebridge.'

'But we can't!' protested Robyn, in a strangled voice, almost forgetting that they had an audience, but Ben soon reminded her.

'Why not?' he demanded impatiently. 'Of course you'll stay here. It's your home. Where else would you go?'

Robyn made an effort to clear her throat. 'It—it's very kind of you—both,' she said, almost choking on the words, 'but I'm sorry. I—we—can't accept.'

'Don't be silly, Robyn!' A patronising note was creeping into her father-in-law's voice now. 'Your staying here has never been in question.'

'Not to you, maybe,' said Robyn doggedly, avoiding Jared's inimical stare. 'But—but ever since—since Stephen died——'

'Don't you mean, since I came home?' inserted Jared coldly. 'Ever since I came home, you've had to face the possibility of leaving.'

'No.' Robyn held up her head. 'No, that's not what I mean.'

'In any event, this conversation is unnecessary,' declared Ben, his gnarled fingers clasping and unclasping over the arm of his chair with increasing agitation. 'You're staying, and that's an end of it. This house is big enough, goodness knows. And, if Jared does get married, and his wife doesn't want to share the house with another woman, we'll face that problem when it comes.'

'No——'

'I'm afraid it has to be yes,' said Jared evenly. 'That's the condition I'm making. That you and Dan stay here. I like the boy, and I think he likes me. I want to know him better. It'll be good for him to have a younger man in his life. He needs a father. Surely you wouldn't deprive me of the chance to get to know my own—nephew?'

CHAPTER FIVE

'IS UNCLE JARED going to stay? Is he? Is he? Grandpa says he is, but you said he wasn't.'

Daniel looked innocently up at her from the soapy depths of his bath, and Robyn felt a desolate pang of desperation. Was there no escape from Jared? Was there no place in this house where she could be free of his pervading influence? Even her son seemed determined to force her into the ignominious position of defending her beliefs, and she had no doubt that, given the alternatives, Daniel would opt for staying here.

'I—don't know,' she said now, wiping a sudsy bubble from her sleeve. 'Daniel, stop splashing about like that! You're wetting the floor, and I don't want to have to get changed again.'

Daniel sniffed, rubbing his nose with a soapy finger. 'You don't want him to, do you?' he accused her unhappily. 'Ever since Uncle Jared came back you've been ever so crotchety.'

'I have *not* been crotchety——'

'Yes, you have.' Daniel hunched his shoulders. 'I just wish I knew why. Why don't you like him?'

'Liking or not liking him has nothing to do with it,' exclaimed Robyn, not altogether truthfully. 'I just think that—well, now that—Uncle Jared has come home, we don't belong here any more.'

Daniel's jaw sagged. 'Did he say that?'

'No. Oh, no.' Robyn couldn't bring herself to actually lie to her son. 'But—well, surely you can see, this is Uncle Jared's home now, and if he gets married and has a family of his own...'

'...he won't want us here any more,' finished Daniel miserably. 'Oh, cripes! I never thought of that.'

69

'No, well—you wouldn't, would you?' Robyn sighed, wishing they had never started this conversation. 'Now— have you washed behind your ears?'

'Hmm.' Daniel was thoughtful and, propping one elbow on his knee, he cupped his chin in a soapy hand. 'But—couldn't we stay here until Uncle Jared gets married?' he asked hopefully. 'I mean, it could be ages and ages, couldn't it? We don't have to leave straight away, do we?'

'You don't have to leave at all,' declared a voice from the doorway that Robyn was rapidly growing to hate. Turning her head, she found Jared propped against the frame and, absorbed as she had been in the effort of preventing Daniel from soaking her suit, she had no way of knowing how long he had been standing there. She had thought when she had escaped upstairs, ostensibly to supervise her son's bath, that any further discussion of that particular subject this evening might be avoided. But evidently Jared had come upstairs to get changed, and he was not above eavesdropping if he thought it might prove beneficial.

Ignoring her son's delighted face, Robyn got quickly to her feet. 'That's not true,' she said, realising she could not allow this to go on a moment longer. 'I'm sorry, Daniel.' She cast a regretful glance over her shoulder at the boy, before confronting Jared's enigmatic gaze. 'We'll stay at Saddlebridge until Christmas. After that, Daniel and I will be moving into our own home.'

Jared's lips thinned. 'Will you?'

The menace was evident behind the casually spoken words, and it took a great effort for Robyn not to be intimidated by it. 'I think so, yes,' she managed stiffly. 'I'm—I'm grateful for the offer, but I really can't accept.'

'But why not, Mum?'

Daniel's cry of disappointment was a faint echo of the cold determination in Jared's voice. 'Yes, why not?' he asked implacably. 'It's what I want; it's what Dan wants; it's what my father wants. Are you seriously thinking of taking a sick man's only grandson away from him?'

'You—*devil!*'

Robyn had her back to Daniel, so the mouthed words were not visible to him, but Jared could read them, and his lips twisted malevolently.

'Such language!' he mocked in an undertone, and then, raising the level of his words, he added, 'I'm so glad you're giving the matter some thought. It does seem foolish to move away from Saddlebridge when there's absolutely no need.'

'Oh—*great!*'

Daniel's excitement caused great scoops of water to spill on to the bathroom floor and, on the pretext of asking Janet for a towel to soak the overflow up, Robyn strode towards the door. She was tempted to try and force her way past Jared, but the idea of challenging his superior strength deterred her. Instead, she stopped in front of him, her desired intentions evident, and with an infuriatingly mocking smile he stepped aside.

She halted half-way through the door, however, and, endeavouring to control her anger, she advised Daniel to get out of the bath and start drying himself. 'I shall expect you to be in bed in fifteen minutes,' she added, aware of the resentful note in her voice, but unable to do anything about it. 'You hear?'

'Yes, Mum,' said Daniel glumly, his enthusiasm doused. Telling herself that her anger was justified, Robyn walked quickly towards the stairs.

However, after informing Janet of the spillage, Robyn did not return to the bathroom. Instead, she went to her own suite of rooms, wishing she could close the door on her troubles as easily as she could close the door of her room. No matter which way she turned, Jared seemed able to thwart her, and when it came to her son, she dared not run the risk of Jared using an old indiscretion against her.

An old indiscretion? She shook her head, as she moved away from the door. Was that all it had been? Certainly, it had been a mistake, a terrible mistake, and one she had suffered from for the whole of her married life.

And yet, before it had happened, her relationship with Jared had been so different. From the very beginning, when she had first come to live at Saddlebridge, they had been good friends. Of course, Jared had only been thirteen years old when she came to live here, and she supposed his liking for her had been not dissimilar to Daniel's liking for Jared. Perhaps he had even had a crush on her, she admitted, feeling a constriction in her throat. In any event, he had made her feel this was her home in a way Stephen, away at college at that time, had never done. In fact, in those early days, she had resented the times when Stephen was at home and Jared had deserted her for more boyish pursuits. That was in the days before Stephen really noticed her and, remembering now, she had to admit that what Joan Hedley had said was true. She had been fond of Jared then— but only as an older sister was fond of a brother, she amended swiftly. She had not been attracted to him, not at all; it would have been ludicrous.

Nevertheless, as Jared grew older, she had been aware that his attitude towards her was changing. His sixteenth birthday had been a case in point, and she remembered very clearly the kiss they had exchanged in the morning-room at Saddlebridge. At twenty-one, she had considered herself very mature and, after giving Jared the gift she had bought for him, it had seemed the most natural thing in the world to lean forward and kiss his cheek. But Jared had turned his head—deliberately, she now knew—and instead of brushing the newly roughening skin of his cheek, her lips had encountered the parted sensuality of his mouth. She flinched even now at the memory of that blatant caress. For some ridiculous reason, she hadn't drawn back as soon as she discovered her mistake. Instead, she had let him step nearer to her, and the warm invasion of his tongue against her teeth had turned her limbs to water.

Of course, she had been able to rationalise it later. It was around the time when she was first becoming attracted to Stephen, and it had been a simple matter to persuade herself that the brothers were sufficiently alike for her to have mistaken one for the other. In any case, anything else would have been totally humiliating, and she had made sure never to make the same mistake again.

And, in spite of her misgivings, her relationship with Jared was not permanently impaired. On the contrary, she missed him terribly a couple of years later when he went away to university, and even Stephen's increasing interest couldn't quite compensate for Jared's absence.

Well, not immediately, she acknowledged quickly. Not having Jared for her partner at tennis, or missing his companionship when she went riding, was soon forgotten when Stephen asked her to marry him. He had been home from college for some time then, and lost no time in staking his claim to her affections, so their engagement was announced at Christmas, and the wedding planned for the middle of May the following year.

She knew Stephen's father had been delighted at the prospect of making her a real member of the family at last, but she had never suspected that he might have had some part in Stephen's decision. It was not until afterwards that her doubts were conceived, and by then it was too late to do anything about it. Besides, she had initially blamed herself for Stephen's indiscretions. She was firmly convinced that she had been the cause.

Pressing her palms together, Robyn allowed the recollection of the events that had precipitated that guilt to sweep over her. She had been such a fool, she remembered bitterly. She should have known better than to trust Jared after what had gone before. But the truth was, she had felt a little sorry for him and, because Stephen was away, she had fallen into his trap.

The sequence of events which had changed her life had begun at Christmas, she acknowledged. It was Jared's first holiday at home since he had gone away to Oxford, and his attitude towards her then should have warned her he was no longer the boy who had gone away. She went to meet his train in Sheffield, and she was astonished at the change in him. He was thinner and taller and, with a day's growth of beard on his chin, he was also extremely attractive.

Even so, after a moment's initial embarrassment over the kiss they exchanged—the abrasive brush of his chin against her cheek had been absurdly intimate—Robyn soon found herself talking to him quite easily, dropping back into the casual camaraderie of Jared's pre-college days without too much difficulty. They talked about the university, and his father; they even laughed about her efforts to organise a Christmas pageant at the church; and it wasn't until she started bringing Stephen's name into the conversation that she noticed a certain sense of withdrawal in Jared's attitude. She didn't mention the proposed engagement, which was to take place on Christmas Eve. Although she knew it was foolish, she was curiously loath to admit that to him. Instead, she talked of other things, and despised her lack of courage.

For Stephen's part, he treated his brother with the same air of condescension he had always adopted. He had always used the six years there were between them to sustain his authority, as if he knew that allowing Jared to get beneath his guard would defeat his seniority. In consequence, he saw nothing amiss in Jared's behaviour, probably assuming Jared's new aloofness was an acknowledgement of his own superiority.

But Jared wasn't stupid, and Robyn knew that he had immediately guessed that things had changed. She saw him watching her and Stephen together, and she knew he suspected what had happened. But even so, he said nothing, and because she was a coward, Robyn said nothing, too.

A few days before Christmas, she held the final rehearsal for the pageant. Most of the participants were boys and girls from the village school, and Robyn had devised a colourful display incorporating the traditional scenes of the nativity into a medieval tableau. The children's parents had spent weeks designing the costumes and, set against the turreted backcloth Robyn had painted, the effect was quite enchanting.

It was Ben who suggested she should take Jared along to the rehearsal. 'Didn't you say you were having some problem with the spotlights?' he'd asked, at dinner the night before. 'Let Jared have a look at them. It will give him something to do. And,' he paused, 'it might persuade him to shave.'

Jared's unwillingness to use his razor at least once a day was causing a growing rift to develop between him and his father, and Robyn wished Ben wouldn't use her to get back at his son.

Nevertheless, Jared had shaved when he appeared at lunch the following day. 'What time are we leaving?' he asked, seating himself opposite her at the table in the morning-room; and, not for the first time, Robyn wished that Stephen and his father did not take their midday meal at the mill.

'You don't have to come, you know,' she murmured, serving herself from the bowl of beef broth Janet had set between them. 'As a matter of fact, the spotlights are fixed. Simon Heslop mended the fuse on Tuesday. If that's the reason you're coming, there's really no need. I'm sure you've got better things to do than watch a lot of children falling over themselves.'

'Like what?' Jared asked quietly, his green gaze steadily on hers.

'Well——' Robin lifted her shoulders helplessly '—don't you have people—*friends* you want to see? I can think of a dozen girls who'd jump at the chance to spend the afternoon with you,' she added somewhat patronisingly, and then wished she hadn't when his gaze never wavered.

'But not you,' he remarked, looking at her over the rim of the soup spoon he was raising to his mouth.

'I didn't say that.' She was flustered, and it showed, and she wondered when he had acquired this capacity to disconcert her like this. He hadn't used to be so unpredictable. But then, she had never really had anything to hide.

'So—I'll come with you, if you'll have me,' he appended drily, and she managed a thin smile.

'Oh—of course,' she agreed, dragging her eyes away from his and concentrating on the soup in her plate. At least they would not be alone, she reminded herself grimly. One of the advantages—or disadvantages, depending on your point of view—of working with children, was their ability to be everywhere at once. There was no facility for privacy at the church hall, and Simon Heslop, the vicar's curate, was unlikely to permit Jared to threaten his authority.

What Robyn had not taken into account was the drive to and from the village hall. It would have been stupid to take two cars, so they used the Range Rover Ben kept for the bad weather. It was natural, therefore, that Jared should drive, and Robyn sat beside him, wondering why she felt so on edge.

The rehearsal was a complete fiasco. The children playing Mary and Joseph could do nothing but giggle all the way through, and it was obvious that Simon, who played the Lord of Misrule, had forgotten his lines. Robyn found her temper increasingly difficult to control and, although she knew it was just an amateur presentation and that the audience would be hopelessly partisan, she couldn't help feeling impatient and letting her feelings show.

By the time they left the church hall, she was ridiculously near to tears, and it didn't help when Jared chided her for her behaviour. 'They're only kids, you know,' he remarked, as they left the lights of the village behind and turned on to the private road that marked the boundary of Saddlebridge. 'They want to have fun, not produce a performance to rival Olivier's! It's only a village pageant, Robyn—not *Twelfth Night*!'

'Of course, you *would* say that!' she countered, needing a whipping boy, and he was there. 'Naturally, *I* can't hope to compete with anything you're likely to see at Oxford, but I take this seriously, and I resent being made to look a fool!'

'You didn't look a fool,' said Jared flatly. 'In fact, as an amateur production, it's pretty good——'

'Talk about being damned with faint praise!' Robyn interrupted bitterly and, with an oath and a squeal of brakes, Jared brought the four-wheeled vehicle to a standstill.

They were still about half a mile from the house, on the narrow country road that circled Saddlebridge, and Robyn looked about her anxiously as the engine died, wishing she had had the sense to keep her arguments to herself until they were safely home.

'Now,' said Jared, switching on the interior light, and half turning in his seat to face her. 'Why don't we discuss what this is really about? Steve's asked you to marry him, hasn't he? Why don't you come right out and admit it?'

Robyn's lips parted. 'I—well, what if he has? What has it got to do with you?'

'Oh, come on.' Jared was impatient now. 'I guess you've been waiting for me to get home to give lover-boy your decision.' His fingers, resting on the back of her seat, suddenly stroked her neck and she flinched in sudden alarm. 'You know you can't marry him, don't you, Robyn?' he added, his voice incredibly sensual. 'That would be a crazy thing to do, wouldn't it? You're not in love with him.'

Robyn was absolutely stunned. She had known Jared might not be enthusiastic about her engagement to Stephen, but she had never dreamt he might mount an all-out attack. Good heavens, she thought incredulously, any minute now he's going to tell me I love him instead!

The idea was so ludicrous, she knew she had to stop him before he said something he would later regret. Obviously, he considered one term at Oxford had given him the ability to interpret her feelings in a totally subjective way, but, unless she prevented him from going any further, the situation between them would become intolerable.

'As—as a matter of fact, you're wrong,' she got out quickly. 'I—I do love Stephen. And—he knows it. It's a secret really, but I know he won't mind if I tell you. We—er—we're getting engaged on Christmas Eve.'

The remainder of the Christmas break was something of an anticlimax after that. In spite of the excitement of her engagement, Robyn couldn't forget Jared's expression when she had told him she was going to marry his brother. He had looked—*stricken*; that was the only word she could think of to describe his face. Although she told herself she had had no choice but to break the news to him, she still felt absurdly responsible for ruining his holiday.

Even so, it had had to be done, and when, two days into the New Year, Jared suddenly announced he was going to spend the rest of the holiday with some friends in Switzerland, Robyn mentally breathed a sigh of relief. Jared would soon find someone else with whom to console himself, she told herself firmly, and dismissed the fleeting trace of irritation she felt at this prospect as simple possessiveness.

It wasn't so easy to make excuses for herself when Jared failed to come home at all at Easter. She didn't want to be the cause of banishing him from his home but, short of confiding her fears to Stephen, there was nothing she could do about it.

And then, about a month before the wedding, Jared did come home. Stephen was away at the time in South America, visiting their suppliers in Brazil and Argentina, and when word was sent by his tutor that Jared had contracted bronchitis his father sent a reluctant Robyn to Oxford to bring him home for rest and recuperation.

'God knows what he's been doing,' Ben had told her tersely, his expression a mixture of irritability and concern. 'According to this chap, Fellowes, he's only narrowly avoided getting pneumonia. Go and fetch him, Robyn. He's more likely to come if you ask him. Tell him I expect him to spend at least two weeks at home, and I won't listen to any excuses.'

Robyn tried to protest that he should make the request personally, but Ben always had an excuse. 'I can't leave the mill to run itself,' he argued firmly, 'what with Stephen being away and all. Don't let me down on this, Robyn. I thought you had a soft spot for him yourself.'

And so Robyn drove down to Oxford with David McCloud, and persuaded a curiously apathetic Jared that he would recover that much quicker at home, with his family to look after him. He seemed indifferent, and the journey back to Saddlebridge was decidedly awkward. Ever since that exchange in the Range Rover, there had been a definite barrier between them, and, although she kept telling herself that once she and Stephen were married things would be different, she didn't quite believe it.

Once they arrived at Saddlebridge, Janet took one look at Jared's thin pale face and insisted he went straight to bed, and for the next few days Robyn saw nothing of him. She knew how he was progressing because Ben spent a lot of time with his son, but personally she was quite happy to keep out of his way.

Then, one morning towards the end of the week, Jared came into the library where Robyn was writing some letters. It was an unusually bright morning, after a week of almost continuous rain, and a clump of late daffodils were daring to raise their heads outside. The lawns, too, had benefited from their thorough soaking, and were greener than before. There were lambs in the fields beyond the paddock, and the sun was glinting brilliantly off the rocks of Saddleford Tor.

'Oh...' Robyn looked up in some confusion at her brother-in-law-to-be's appearance. Only last night, Ben had confided in her that he was worried about his son's apparent indifference to his recovery, and to see Jared standing there before her, pale maybe, but unquestionably fitter than he had been, was quite unnerving. 'Are you feeling better?'

'Some,' agreed Jared evenly, crossing the room to the window, to stand with his hands in the pockets of his black suede trousers, staring out on to the burgeoning life of the garden. He was wearing a black sweater, too, that accentuated the extreme lightness of his hair; seated at the desk, Robyn found her eyes were irresistibly drawn to the arrowing of silvery-blonde hair that brushed the neckline of the woollen garment. She remembered feeling an almost tangible desire to touch that vulnerable part of his anatomy, and she had to drag her eyes away and concentrate on the letter she was writing.

'What are you doing?' he asked at last, turning to face her, and once again she was obliged to keep a strict hold on her emotions.

'Nothing much,' she remarked dismissively. 'Writing to a schoolfriend, that's all.' She omitted to mention that the schoolfriend in question was to be one of her brides-maids when she married Stephen.

'Want to go for a ride?' he enquired unexpectedly, and she caught her breath.

'To go for a ride?' she echoed disbelievingly. 'But— you can't! You've been in bed for the best part of a week!'

'I haven't.' Jared came to stand in front of the desk, and she was dismayed to find the hot colour was flooding into her cheeks under his cool appraisal. 'I've just been keeping out of the way, that's all.'

Robyn swallowed. 'What do you mean?'

'I thought that was what you wanted.'

'What *I* wanted?'

'Well, you haven't exactly fallen over yourself to find out if I was OK, have you?'

Robyn wet her lips with a nervous tongue. 'Your father——' she began, and with a twisted smile Jared inclined his head.

'Oh, yes. My father's kept you informed.'

'Well, he has.'

'I'm not arguing, am I?' Jared sighed. 'So—OK. Will you go for a ride with me?'

'On—on horseback?'

'Well, I don't mean in the Range Rover,' remarked Jared drily, and she felt her breathing quicken alarmingly.

'I—don't think your father would—approve,' she said at last, and Jared uttered an imprecation.

'I'm not a child, Robyn, even if you'd prefer me to act that way. I'm all right, I tell you. I'm a bit weak, but who wouldn't be after swallowing gallons of Janet's chicken broth and little else? What I need is some exercise, and some fresh air. Now—are you going to come with me, or do I have to go on my own?'

'You can't go on your own.'

Robyn's response was instinctive, and Jared arched his brows quizzically. 'Well?'

'All right.' Much against her better judgement, Robyn agreed to accompany him, and fifteen minutes later they were clattering out of the stable yard and on to the open moorland behind the house.

In fact, she enjoyed herself enormously. It was months since she had done more than exercise the bay mare Ben had bought her for her twenty-first birthday—not since Jared had gone away to college, she realised ruefully— and it was marvellous to get right away from the house, and give the spirited animal its head. On top of this, the air was pure and clear, like wine—and, like wine, it was intoxicating.

By the time they cantered back to the stables, she realised that for the past hour she had forgotten the reasons why she and Jared had spent so little time together at Christmas. The morning had passed without any tension or cross words between them and, seeing the healthy colour glowing in Jared's lean features, she felt an answering glow of achievement that she had had some part in his recovery.

That evening, she and Jared had dinner together. Ben was spending the evening at his club in Leeds and, over smoked salmon pâté and a creamy fricassee of chicken, they renewed their old friendship. Of course, Stephen's name didn't figure too strongly in their conversation, although Robyn did express regret that her fiancé would not get to see his brother on this occasion. Jared made some remark about the demands of running a business and the subject was abandoned. If Robyn recognised a certain reticence in his manner, she was happy enough to have avoided another unpleasant scene.

And, during the days that followed, she began to wonder if she had imagined the things he had said to her on that never-to-be-forgotten ride home from the church hall. Jared was so nice to her, so much *fun!* And she was guiltily aware that she wasn't missing Stephen at all.

The weather remained dry and mild, and most mornings they took the horses out for their daily exercise. Jared's father initially expressed the hope that his son was not running the risk of further pulmonary complications by overdoing things, but the evident improvement in Jared's condition was all the proof he needed that this was not so.

It was arranged that Jared should return to Oxford at the end of the following week; he had spoken to his tutor on the phone and assured him that all was well. As his time at home drew to a close, Robyn knew a quite unwarranted feeling of depression. She told herself it was because Stephen was still away, and that as soon as her fiancé returned home she would feel altogether different, but for the time being, nothing could alter the fact that she was dreading Jared's departure.

They spent the Friday before he left in Sheffield, doing last-minute shopping for things Jared was needing. The doctor had suggested that wearing a T-shirt under a sweater might prevent his catching another similar chill, which had almost turned to pneumonia, and although Robyn suspected he'd never wear them she insisted on his buying half a dozen to take back to college. The doctor had also recommended that he should wear a pyjama jacket, as well as trousers, to sleep in, and although Jared protested that he had plenty of pyjamas at home, Robyn bought him two new pairs in Marks and Spencer's. She was perfectly aware that the expensive silk pyjamas he had at home had never seen the light of day—or night—in Oxford, but perhaps something more practical might convince him of their value.

It was quite late when they got back to Saddlebridge. They had called for a drink on the way home, and it was after six when they reached the house. However, there was no sign of Ben's Rolls-Royce, and Janet met them with the news that Mr Morley was dining with his accountant.

'He's given David the night off,' she added. 'He says if he decides to come home, he'll get a taxi. If not, he might spend the night at his club.'

'Oh.' Robyn acknowledged this news with an unforgivable sense of anticipation. At least she would not have to spend the evening steering Ben's conversation away from his elder son. And she and Jared would be able to talk, without the confining influence of his father.

'No sweat,' said Jared now, evidently misinterpreting Robyn's sudden silence. 'Hey, why don't you take the evening off, too, Janet? Rob and I can fend for ourselves. We might even go out. Isn't that right, Robyn?'

'What?' Robyn endeavoured to concentrate on what he had said. 'Oh—yes.' She gave Janet a warm smile. 'Why don't you? Take the evening off, I mean. You and your husband could go out somewhere, if you wanted. You know Ben won't mind if you borrow the car.'

Janet's lips tilted. 'You know, we might just do that.' She hesitated. 'If you're sure you and Jared——'

'We're not completely helpless,' said Jared drily. 'Go on. Enjoy yourselves. Believe me, at college I usually make do with a burger.'

'But you're not at college now,' murmured Janet doubtfully. 'And your father——'

'My father's not here,' declared Jared flatly. 'There's just Rob and me. And we're giving you the evening off. Are you going to turn us down?'

Of course, after that, Janet could hardly refuse. Besides, it was obvious she wanted to take them at their word and, by the time Robyn excused herself to take her own purchases upstairs, Janet was on her way to their apartments at the back of the house to tell her husband the good news.

Putting the tights and make-up she had bought away in her drawers, Robyn couldn't prevent the little frisson of excitement that ran up her spine at the thought that she and Jared were going to be alone in the house. It was ridiculous, and she was certainly old enough to know better, but he was an attractive man—*boy*, she corrected herself severely—and it was flattering to know that he enjoyed her company rather than that of someone of his own age. Of course, it was possible that there was someone back at college he would rather be with, but that was not something on which she allowed her mind to linger. Instead, she turned her efforts to reminding herself that she was to be married in a little over three weeks, and that fantasising about Jared was both dangerous and juvenile.

She heard the Rolls-Royce purr away down the drive as she was trying out the new dusky pink eye-shadow she had discovered in Rackham's. The tyres crunching over the gravel brought her surreptitiously to her window, and she peered round the curtains with a definite feeling of stimulation.

Curbing her anticipation, Robyn left the window and returned to her experimentation. For heaven's sake, she scolded herself severely, she had spent the weeks between Christmas and Jared's unexpected homecoming despising him for trying to come between her and Stephen. And now, here she was, acting like a schoolgirl because they were to spend the evening alone in the house.

Putting the suddenly offensive eye-shadow aside, she stared at her reflection. What she saw, delectable as it was, did not please her. Her eyes were brilliant, there was becoming colour in her cheeks, and the glossy curtain of her hair gleamed with good health. She did not look like a girl who was pining for the fiancé who had been away for the better part of three weeks. She looked like someone's mistress, waiting for her lover, and that was a situation she could not allow to proceed. The last thing she wanted was for Jared to think she was attracted to him. The safest course would be for them to go out for the evening, too. That way, they would have other people around them, and no opportunity to tread on dangerous territory.

It was so silly, really, she thought, as she went downstairs. It wasn't as if she was highly sexed or anything. She had had no difficulty whatsoever in sustaining her innocence throughout her relationship with Stephen, although she acknowledged that his reticence stemmed more from a desire not to annoy his father than from any particular consideration for her feelings. Even so, he had respected her desire not to anticipate their marriage, and she innocently believed that since their engagement there had been no one else.

She paced about the library for a good half-hour, waiting for Jared to put in an appearance and, by the time she lost patience and went looking for him, she had forgotten her earlier apprehension over the dangers of their relationship.

Instead, after making a tour of Ben's study and the morning-room, and even looking into the kitchen to see if he was there, she made her way back up the stairs again, taking the corridor to his room without even turning a hair.

She knocked at his door with rather more hesitation, but, on receiving no answer, she speedily knocked again. 'Jared,' she called, wondering, somewhat belatedly, if anything could be wrong. 'Jared! Are you in there? Come on. Can't you answer the door?'

'Coming!'

The lazy response reassured her that at least he was not suffering any after-effects of their trip. But her nails curled into the palms of her hands with impatience as he kept her waiting several more seconds before opening the door.

When he did she felt an instantaneous surge of some emotion she didn't care to identify. Instead of the jeans and sweater he had worn to go shopping in Sheffield, he had on one of the thin shirts they had bought there, and beneath his dark blue underwear his long legs were bare.

'Oh—sorry about this,' he said carelessly, and she knew, infuriatingly, that he was aware of her disconcertment. 'I've just had a shower, and when you knocked I wasn't dressed. D'you want to come in? I shan't be a second.'

Robyn shook her head. 'No—I—that is, I just thought perhaps we should go out tonight.' She moistened her lips. 'What do you think?'

'Should?'

Jared was too astute, and Robyn coloured. 'All right—*might*, then,' she amended tersely. 'I thought we *might* go out tonight. As—as Janet's gone out.'

'We're alone, I know,' said Jared drily, turning back into the room. 'Look—do you mind closing that door? I know this house is centrally heated, but I have just had a shower, and there's quite a draught from the hall.'

Robyn hesitated. 'But, well—what do you think?'

Jared turned his head. 'I think you're scared of being alone with me,' he retorted flatly. 'But—OK. If that's the way you want it.'

Robyn took a deep breath and stepped into the room, closing the door behind her. 'I am not scared of being alone with you,' she declared, although her hand still lingered on the handle. 'And—and if you believe going around half naked is likely to embarrass me, you couldn't be more wrong. You forget—I've known you since you were a toddler! And you used to wear a lot less than that to swim in the pool!'

'Ah,' Jared's lips twisted. 'But you have to admit, I am bigger now,' he remarked mockingly. 'I remember you, too, Robyn. And you were always afraid to take a chance.'

'That's not true!'

'It is true,' he said, turning back to her, and she had to force her eyes not to move from the open V of olive skin visible above the neckline of his shirt. 'You always took the safest way out of any situation. That's why you've let Steve and my father browbeat you into this engagement. You knew it was what my father wanted, and because you felt so grateful to him for taking you in when your parents were killed, you never even hesitated when Steve popped the question.'

'That is not true!' Robyn swallowed convulsively. 'I love Stephen.'

'Do you?' Jared took the steps necessary to leave only a foot of space between them. 'Is that why you're trembling like a leaf because you're afraid I'm going to touch you?'

Robyn quivered. 'You flatter yourself!'

'No, I don't.' Jared made no move to touch her, but continued to regard her with lazily sensual eyes. 'I just know a little more about this feeling there is between us. I know what it means, and I'm tempted to show you what it means, too.'

Robyn's breathing quickened. 'You have no shame, do you? You know I'm your brother's fiancée, and yet you stand there——'

'—half naked——' he inserted sardonically.

'—and tell me there's something between us.'

'There is.'

'There isn't!'

'Do you want me to prove it?'

'No. I mean——' Robyn was pressing herself back against the door so hard, her shoulderblades ached '—there's nothing to prove. Except your disloyalty to your brother. And—and to me.'

'Don't talk such utter crud!' exclaimed Jared harshly, moving to rest one hand on either side of her as she pressed herself against the door. 'Where's the point in being loyal, when the woman I love is doing her level best to ruin both our lives?'

He was so close now, she could feel the warmth of his body, smell the aroma of the soap he used. She sensed the heated urgency of his emotions and acknowledged the need to fight against a temptation quite as old as time.

'You—you don't love me, Jared,' she got out unsteadily.

'Don't I?' His eyes dipped to rest on the rapid rise and fall of her breasts, apparent beneath the finely knit wool of her sweater.

'No, I—Jared, stop doing that! I'm trying to discuss this sensibly, and you're deliberately trying to disconcert me.'

'How am I trying to do that?' enquired Jared softly, and she despised the way his husky voice scraped across her senses. 'I haven't even touched you.'

'Just—stop looking at me like that,' exclaimed Robyn tremulously. 'And—and put some clothes on. If—if anyone was to come in here now——'

'Yes?' Jared arched one enquiring brow.

'Well—what would they think?'

Jared half smiled. 'The same old argument, hmm, Robyn? I'm behaving naturally, and you can't stand it.'

'You are *not* behaving naturally!' she told him unsteadily. 'You're taking advantage of—of a situation. If your father knew——'

'Oh, yes, I wondered when that was coming.' Jared's mouth curled. 'If my father knew, he'd thrash me, is that what you think? Well, sorry, Robyn, but I don't think my father could do that any more. Whether you believe it or not, I am not a boy any longer.'

Robyn swallowed. 'Then stop behaving like one.'

'OK, I will.' He straightened abruptly, releasing her from the prison his arms had created. 'Go on. Get out of here. I don't need the aggravation.'

Robyn shifted away from the door with some relief but, now that she was free to go, she was curiously loath to do so. She didn't want them to part on this note; she didn't want Jared to return to Oxford with the remembrance of this scene as his companion. Things had been so good between them these past days, and she wanted them to remain that way. How she wished she had never started this; but she had, and she had to finish it.

'Jared...' she began awkwardly, as he snatched up a pair of dark grey trousers and started putting them on. 'Jared, please! I want us to be friends.'

'Friends?' He didn't even look at her. 'I can't be your friend, Robyn. You and I have nothing more to say to one another.'

'That's not true.'

He turned to look at her then, pushing the hem of his shirt into his trousers as he did so. 'Will you stop saying that?' he snarled, and she had to force her eyes not to follow the movements of his hands. 'I know what I'm saying, believe me. And if you want me to remember that you are Steve's fiancée, and I'm only your brother-in-law-to-be, you'd better leave, right now!'

Robyn sighed, taking an involuntary step towards him. 'Jared,' she began again, 'Jared, it needn't be this way...'

'Needn't it?' Jared's face was a guarded mask, but Robyn was too intent on what he was saying to pay a lot of attention to visible danger signals.

'No,' she persisted, her confidence growing when he didn't immediately rebuff her. 'Look—we've had a good time this week, haven't we? We've had some fun. We always have fun. We like doing the same things. Jared, how can we not be friends when we enjoy being together?'

Almost without being aware of it, she had narrowed the space between them as she spoke. Now, there was scarcely an arm's length between them and, although that knowledge was a little intimidating, Robyn couldn't move back again without losing her advantage.

There was silence for a long moment, but instead of easing the tension it seemed to heighten it. The air between them seemed to vibrate with it, and Robyn, who had been convinced she could convince him, was suddenly equally as convinced she couldn't. She didn't trust his silence; she didn't trust the abnormal stillness that surrounded him; and when he expelled his breath on a long sigh, she started at the sound like a frightened gazelle.

But even then she didn't act on her awareness. With Jared's direct green gaze holding hers, she felt a curious paralysis in her limbs, a kind of hypnosis that kept her where she was, even when he put out his hand and rubbed his knuckles down her cheek. The hard brush of his fingers against her flesh was not sufficient to release the awful magnetism that held her, and the years she knew there were between them seemed suddenly reversed. She was the junior, held in thrall by his superior perception; she was the innocent, made helpless by his superior knowledge.

'I did warn you,' he said at last, in a thick voice she hardly recognised. 'I did warn you, Robyn!' And before she could react, he pulled her into his arms, and found her mouth with his with unerring deliberation.

CHAPTER SIX

AFTERWARDS, Robyn had managed to convince herself that Jared had given her no chance to resist. The recollection of what had happened had become confused in her mind, and she had succeeded in persuading herself that Jared had forced himself upon her. What other reason could there have been for what had occurred between them? What other excuse could there be for the way she had behaved? She could not accept that she had willingly betrayed Stephen. That way had led to disaster, and the ruin of their future together.

Today, however, allowing every detail of that evening to ressurrect itself, Robyn could not be so sanctimonious. It had been hypocritical of her to put all the blame on Jared's shoulders. God forgive her, she had not exactly put up much of a fight. From the minute he had touched her, she had been aware it was a losing battle.

But why had she known that? she asked herself now, pacing restlessly about her bedroom. What was there about Jared that had caused her to behave so uncharacteristically? Had she been flattered by his attentions? Had she been so desperate for affection that she had unwittingly encouraged his advances? Goodness knew, she had been aware of his attraction, but objectively, she had thought; like a sister might be aware of a brother.

Perhaps the fact that Jared had evidently had some experience had had something to do with it. At that time, she had assumed he was more experienced than Stephen, and she had despised him for using her as he had so many others. It was only after her marriage that she had discovered her mistake. And then she had dismissed them both as being tarred with the same brush.

But, whatever her subsequent thoughts had been, at the time she had seemingly made only a token effort to resist him. When his lips had touched hers, she had lost the will to fight him, and her awareness of his superior strength had been a convenient vindication.

All the same, he had not kissed her like Stephen kissed her. Her fiancé's soft, wet-lipped caresses were nothing like the firm possession of Jared's mouth. When Stephen kissed her, he breathed into her mouth; Jared, quite simply, took her breath away.

They were both breathing heavily when his lips left hers and sought the sensitive hollow where her neck curved into her shoulder. Pushing the soft collar of her sweater aside, Jared allowed his tongue to search out the quivering softness of her skin, and Robyn's limbs suffused with heat at that unfamiliar invasion. She wasn't used to such intimacies, or to such a sensual approach, and her unsuspecting body was contributing to her betrayal.

She remembered saying, 'No, Jared!' or 'We can't do this,' or some such thing, but her protests were as unconvincing as her response was positive. In any case, Jared wasn't listening to her. He was intent on arousing emotions she had not even known she possessed at that time, and his hands left her shoulders to seek the narrow contours of her hips.

He drew her hard against him, against the rigid bones of his pelvis, and the unmistakable thrust of his manhood rising between. The pulsating throb against her stomach seemed to ridicule her claims that he was still a boy, and the potent pressure of his body seemed to turn her bones to water. He was so lean and strong and masculine; so *young*, she acknowledged now, with a bitter grimace. But old in the ways of making love, she added grimly. While she had been just a novice in comparison.

Even so, when his mouth had returned to hers, she had been ready and eager to accommodate him. However much she might despise herself now, she had not repulsed his escalating passion. On the contrary, she had been more than willing to part her lips and allow the intimate invasion of his tongue. And once she felt that intrusion, moist and sensuous, stroking the sensitive places of her mouth, she had realised how treacherous her own senses could be.

She didn't remember how they got to the bed, she only remembered the feeling of softness against her bare skin. The buttons of her sweater had posed no obstacle to Jared's searching hands, and the heat of his body against her flesh was a natural escalation. He had cupped her breasts in his hands, she recalled shudderingly, taking each of them to his lips in turn, caressing their tips with his tongue and turning her bones to water. She hadn't been frigid then; she had been hot and eager and shameless, meeting his forbidden passion with an urgency she could hardly understand now, letting him have his way and encouraging him to do so.

Maybe her eyes had been closed, she thought now; maybe she had succeeded in convincing herself that it was Stephen who was making love to her. But, whatever her excuse at the time, afterwards she had never experienced such a lack of inhibition again. Afterwards, she had lost the ability to feel such emotions surging inside her, and there was no one to blame but Jared for her arrested sensibilities.

She shook her head bitterly. If only she had known what she was inviting, she thought. If only she had perceived what those heated moments of passion would cost her! But at the time, she had been too bemused to think of anything, too much at the mercy of her senses to consider anything so nebulous as the future.

Had her eyes been closed when she had helped Jared shed his clothes? she asked herself scornfully. Had she not seen his hands slide the close-fitting jeans from her own body, and follow their passage with his lips? Had her legs not parted to the sensuous brush of his tongue against her inner thigh? And had she not grasped his hair and brought his lips to hers again in a fever of blind infatuation?

Of course she had done all those things. She had arched her back and rubbed herself against his lean hard strength. She had even found the urge to touch him quite irresistible, and she could still recall the feel of his pulsating maleness in her hands.

Jared had said, 'Oh, God!' and 'Robyn!' in a choked voice, and she had known a never-repeated surge of satisfaction at his evident pleasure in what she was doing. So much so that she had wound her legs about him, and after that there had been no possibility of preventing the inevitable.

Shaking her head now, she tried to put those thoughts away from her, but the memories were unravelling like a long-tangled skein of wool inside her head. No matter how unwelcome the truth might be, she had to accept her share of blame for Jared's irresponsibility, and the knowledge of her guilt was like a worm inside her brain.

The fact that it had never happened again was no vindication. It had happened once, and that was enough. No matter that, for a brief space of time, she had experienced emotions she had never known before or since. What they had done had been unforgivable, and she, as the elder, should have had more sense.

However, at the time, sense had been one thing she was lacking. It had taken the painful experience of Jared's invasion of her body to alert her to the horror of what she was doing, and by then it had been much too late. No matter that his face had expressed his astonishment that she was still a virgin. The damage had been done, and Robyn's remorse had been shattering.

But, although she would have left him then, Jared would not let her. 'Do you think I can let you go now?' he demanded, stilling her struggles with urgent hands. 'Do you think that's all there is to it? Pain?' His lips twisted. 'Oh, Robyn, I have to show you that it's not.'

And, in spite of her initial efforts to thwart him, he did. Although she wanted to break free of him, the hungry brush of his mouth and the caressive touch of his fingers was shamefully pleasurable, and when he started to move, she found herself moving with him. The accelerating thrust of his body was unbearably persuasive, and although she tried to think of Stephen and pretend that it was he who was doing this to her, it became totally impossible. It was Jared whose heated body aroused an answering heat in hers, so that their sweat mingled between them; it was Jared who smoothed the moist hair back from her forehead, and looked down at her with a savage possession, Jared who drove her to the edge of ecstasy, and Jared who held her as the throbbing climax of their mutual release tipped them over into a mindless languor...

Withdrawing now from that unwelcome remembrance, Robyn pressed hot palms to her suddenly burning cheeks. Oh, God, she thought sickly, she hadn't wanted to remember how he had made her feel! Or, afterwards, the overpowering sense of shame she had experienced. She recalled how she had scrambled off the bed while he was still drowsing, evading his lazily extended hand and gathering her scattered clothes together. She hadn't stopped to dress. She had scurried back to her own room like a frightened rabbit, and when Jared eventually came knocking on her door it had been securely locked. She supposed he could have forced his way in, if he had been so determined, but maybe shame at his own actions had restricted his efforts to verbal persuasion. Then, when she had refused to answer him, he had gone away, and it wasn't until the next morning that she had had to face him.

Her lips twisted now. He had actually expected her to break her engagement to Stephen, she remembered tensely. He had even suggested she should wait until he had finished his degree and marry him, and she had taken the greatest pleasure in telling him she wouldn't marry him if he was the last man on earth. She hated him, she despised him, and she told him that, so far as she was concerned, Stephen was worth a *dozen* like him.

If Ben had wondered why his younger son should suddenly pack up and return to college a couple of days earlier than expected, he had made no demur. Besides, he had had word that Stephen would be home at the beginning of the following week, and he expected Robyn, like him, to have more interest in that event.

And she had tried to. Indeed, when Stephen had come home, she had gone out of her way to show him how much she had missed him, and for a few memorable weeks she had been able to persuade herself that nothing monumental had happened. Most girls had had some experience of sex before marriage, and she had decided that Stephen would expect her to be no exception.

Except, that wasn't the end of it. She expelled her breath on a sigh. That was the only beginning. Within two weeks of their wedding, she became convinced that she was pregnant, and the precipitation was such that she knew it couldn't possibly be Stephen's child.

They were on honeymoon at the time that she diagnosed her condition, and the sunlit beauty of the Bahamas became a cruel backdrop to the reality of what had happened. She had thought she was safe. Stephen had been too careless, and too *drunk*, on their wedding night, to notice that she was no longer a virgin, and after satisfying his own needs he had slumped beside her, dead to the world. And, in the days that followed, she had discovered her husband didn't much care whether she participated in his lovemaking or not. So long as she made herself available to him, he was content.

Consequently, the revelation that she was expecting Jared's baby had shocked her to the core, and any hopes she might have had of Stephen's arousing some dormant response inside her was stifled by the stiffness that this horrifying development created. She even considered abortion in those terrifying early days, but eventually she came to realise that the child might be her salvation.

Once they were back in England, it hadn't taken her long to realise how naïve she had been about Stephen's character. She'd soon learned that there were other women in her husband's life, and her own lack of interest in sex was excuse enough, if any was needed, for Stephen to resume his old ways. When she'd eventually plucked up the courage to tell him she was pregnant, it had had no significant effect on his behaviour. Except that he had moved his belongings into the adjoining room, on the pretext of not disturbing her when he came home late at night, and, apart from an occasional visit, he never slept with her again.

There were times in those early days when she determined to tell him the truth, but she never did. He never suspected that Daniel was not his own child. But Jared did, particularly when the baby was born a scant eight months after the wedding. She saw the cold suspicion in his eyes, and for weeks afterwards she lived with the constant fear that he might choose to expose her. But he never did, and when Jared left for Australia she knew an overwhelming sense of relief.

Yet, although she had told herself that Jared's departure would make a difference to her relationship with Stephen, it never did. She soon came to the conclusion that Stephen had wanted her as a wife, but not as a mistress. He liked her; he treated her with affection; but whatever it was he wanted from a woman, it was not the familiarity to be found in his own bed. In consequence, Daniel became the whole focus of her existence, and she learned to dissimulate so well that she almost convinced herself that he *was* Stephen's son.

Of course, eventually, Stephen's affairs became an embarrassment. Initially, she heard of them by the gossip that circulated about him, but inevitably her own friends felt compelled to put her in the picture. After all, they argued, divorce was an acceptable alternative, and these days no woman was expected to put up with that sort of thing. That she had refused even to consider the possibility of a divorce had caused some people to decide that she was either completely stupid, or completely mercenary, but gradually the subject had been dropped. And then, Ben's stroke had created an entirely different situation, and no one expected her to walk out on her commitments any longer, when she was so obviously necessary to the old man's peace of mind.

But it was her own peace of mind that troubled her now. Jared's return, and the ultimatum he had announced only an hour ago in the library, had brought the whole thing back into perspective. Although, on the face of it, his offer sounded genuine enough, she knew it for the compromise it was. Jared was insinuating himself into her life again. He was making himself indispensable to his father, and in the process making himself an integral part of Daniel's future. And how long would he be content to call Daniel his nephew? Wasn't it only a matter of time before he chose to disclose his identity as the boy's father?

Robyn trembled. She felt so helpless. It was all very well insisting that Jared couldn't prove that Daniel was his son, but how would the boy react if he was faced with the possibility? In all honesty, he had had little in common with Stephen, whereas it was obvious that he admired Jared very much. Given that admiration, and the indisputable proof that his characteristics were more those of his father's younger brother, might not Daniel himself turn against her, and how would she bear it if the one person she cared most for in the world blamed her for keeping the truth from him?

She closed her eyes for a moment, unable to face the agony of such a prospect. She could not let it happen; she *must* not let it happen. But how was she going to control a situation that was already getting out of hand?

CHAPTER SEVEN

A WEEK later, Robyn was sleeping a little more easily, and her fears for herself, and Daniel, had been put on an indefinite hold. Jared had returned to Australia two days before, ostensibly to cancel the lease of his apartment in Sydney and tie up his affairs there. He was also to make arrangements to ship his personal belongings to England. As it was only three weeks to Christmas, Robyn was living in hopes that he would decide to spend the festive season in Australia. He had friends and business colleagues in the city, he had told his father so, and it was reasonable to assume that they would want to give him a suitable send-off. Besides, he was bound to have a more exciting time in Sydney than he would at Saddlebridge, and Robyn welcomed the opportunity it would give her to consider her own alternatives.

She received an unexpected invitation a few days after Jared's departure. Mark Kingsley, the new curate at St Peter's, called on Saturday morning to ask if she would be interested in sharing the production of a Christmas pageant with him. 'Mr Tomlinson says that you once helped my predecessor with a similar project,' he confided smilingly. 'I'd be unfailingly grateful if you could give me some advice.'

Mark Kingsley was some years older than his predecessor and, since his arrival in the parish, he had caused quite a stir among the female members of the Reverend Tomlinson's congregation. The fact that he was of a reasonable height and build, with similarly attractive features, and unmarried, made him a regular choice at dinner parties in the neighbourhood, but so far Robyn's association with him had been limited to a perfunctory introduction by the vicar one morning after service.

Now, meeting his appealing gaze, Robyn was absurdly flattered that he should have taken the trouble to ask her. It was years since any man had regarded her in any other capacity than that of Stephen's wife and, although she guessed he would never have approached her without some encouragement from the Reverend Tomlinson, she was tempted. It would be such a relief to be involved with something so *im*personal, and at least it would give her something else to think about.

'I realise you may not want to participate in any celebrations this year, Mrs Morley,' the curate added diffidently. 'I mean—I know it's only a little over two months since Mr Morley died, and—well, if you do feel you would rather not...'

'Oh, no!' Robyn linked her fingers together, holding her arms close against her midriff. 'That is—I'd be delighted to help you, Mr Kingsley.'

'Mark, please,' he amended quickly. 'And I'm delighted, too. When Arnold—that is, Mr Tomlinson, intimated you might be able to offer me some suggestions, I couldn't believe my luck. I've been in the parish over six months and, apart from seeing you in church once or twice, we've never had the opportunity to meet socially.'

'No.' Robyn made a concerted effort to control the wave of unexpected colour that invaded her cheeks. 'I'm afraid, since my father-in-law's illness, we don't entertain much any more.'

'Or accept invitations,' he inserted shrewdly. 'I did meet the late Mr Morley on occasion, but you weren't with him.'

'No.' Robyn's nails dug into her knuckles. 'Well—when do want to start?'

'How about this evening?' said Mark Kingsley at once, and Robyn's eyes widened in surprise. 'At dinner,' he appended. 'I believe the restaurant at The Stag in Ebbersley does quite a good steak.'

Robyn shook her head. 'Oh, but—I couldn't possibly——'

'Why not?' Mark frowned. 'Oh, I see. It's too soon after your husband——'

'No, it's not that.' Robyn's tongue circled her lower lip. 'I just mean—you don't have to take me out to dinner.'

'But I want to,' he replied lightly. 'I've wanted to ask you for weeks. Too many weeks for my own peace of mind, actually.' He grimaced. 'Please. Say you'll accept.'

Robyn was stunned. She had never dreamt that his enquiry might be anything more than an effort on the Reverend Tomlinson's part to get her involved in outside activities once again. So long as Stephen had been alive, she had avoided village gatherings, not least because she knew people were talking about her. Stephen's activities had been common knowledge for so long, and she had never known who was the more embarrassed by her presence, herself or other people.

But now, to receive this unexpected compliment... She didn't know what to say. 'I—it's very kind of you.'

'It's not kind at all,' declared Mark Kingsley firmly. 'You'd make me very happy if you'd accept. What do you say?'

Daniel's appearance at that moment gave her a welcome pause. Her son came bounding down the stairs into the hall with his usual lack of inhibition, and Robyn took the opportunity to reprove him to give herself time to think.

'Um—this is my son, Daniel, Mr Kingsley—*Mark*!' she amended ruefully. And then, with sudden inspiration, she added, 'I wonder, would it be possible for him to be involved in the pageant? I know he doesn't go to the village school or attend Sunday school at the church, but I'm sure he'd be enthusiastic, wouldn't you, darling?'

'Enthusiastic?' Daniel frowned. 'To do what?'

'Mr Kingsley wants me to help him organise a Christmas pageant at the church,' Robyn explained patiently. 'What do you think?'

'Would I get to dress up?' asked Daniel at once, and Mark Kingsley laughed.

'I should think it's a distinct possibility,' he agreed. 'And I can't see any objections to you bringing him along, Mrs Morley. On the contrary, the more the merrier. Which gives me an idea. How does the prospect of Christmas in Sherwood Forest sound to you, Mrs Morley?'

'Oh—please call me Robyn,' she murmured self-consciously, aware that Daniel was watching their exchange with some interest. 'I—er—yes. Yes, that sounds—interesting.'

'Good. We'll discuss it this evening at dinner,' said Mark happily. 'What time shall I pick you up? Would half-past seven suit you?'

'Um——' Conscious that Daniel's ears had pricked up at this unusual occurrence, Robyn quickly decided to give in. 'Er—yes. Half-past seven sounds—fine. I'll look forward to it.'

'So shall I,' endorsed Mark with some satisfaction. 'OK, I'll see you later then, Robyn. Cheerio, Danny. It's been nice meeting you.'

Curiously, however, when the door had closed behind the curate, Daniel was rather less enthusiastic. 'Why didn't you tell him my name's not Danny, it's Daniel?' he demanded, leading the way into the library. 'You always tell Uncle Jared.'

'Oh, well...' Robyn made an indifferent movement of her shoulders. 'That's not important right now. What is, is that it's going to be fun helping to organise the pageant. I organised one years ago. Long before you were born, actually.'

Daniel frowned. 'I still don't see why you didn't tell him——'

'Because it would have been rude, that's why,' declared Robyn impatiently. 'For heaven's sake, Daniel, can't we get off this subject of what Mr Kingsley called you? Don't you think it will be fun getting dressed up? I shall have to look through the old clothes that are in the attic and see if there's something there we can make into an outfit for you.'

Daniel sniffed. 'Why don't we just buy something?' he asked sulkily. 'Besides, I don't know if I want to be in it. Is that Mr Kingsley going to help you? And why did you say he could call you Robyn?'

Robyn sighed. 'It's I who'll be helping him,' she amended firmly. 'And why shouldn't he call me by my Christian name? I'm not that old, Daniel—no matter what you think.'

'I didn't say you were.'

'No, perhaps not.' Robyn shook her head. 'Anyway, as for buying you something to wear, I don't think that's a very good idea. People don't do that sort of thing. All the children's mummies and daddies join in and improvise costumes—that is, they make them up from odds and ends. You don't want to be the odd one out, do you? And I am capable of producing something fairly decent.'

Daniel flung himself into an armchair and propped his chin on one hand. 'Well, I wish Uncle Jared was here, then I could ask him to join in, too,' he declared gloomily. 'Why couldn't he have just asked someone to send his things here, instead of going all the way to Australia just to pack them himself?'

Robyn went to put another log on the fire. 'It wasn't quite that simple,' she said a little tautly, over her shoulder. 'Uncle Jared has an apartment in Sydney, and—lots of friends to say goodbye to. I expect he'll stay there over Christmas, so there's no question of him being involved in the pageant.'

Daniel sniffed again. 'Knickers!'

'*Daniel!*'

'Well...' He was unrepentant. 'I was hoping that during the Christmas holidays he might come sledging with me. Mr McCloud says that he's heard we're going to have a white Christmas. It would have been fun to have someone to play with. Dad never had the time to do anything like that.'

Robyn sucked in her breath. 'Well, you know I'll come sledging with you,' she exclaimed, and Daniel grimaced.

'I know, Mum,' he muttered. 'But it's not the same. All the chaps go with their dads. You know what I mean. Girls aren't the same!'

Robyn forced a faint smile. 'I suppose I should take that as a compliment,' she remarked drily. 'At least you still think of me as a *girl*, not an old lady!'

'Oh, Mum!' Daniel pulled a wry face. 'You're not old. Not really, anyway,' he appended grudgingly. 'But I wish you hadn't said you'd help Mr Kingsley with the pageant. I don't think I like him, and I don't think Uncle Jared will, either.'

'Well, fortunately, what your Uncle Jared thinks or doesn't think is of no concern to me,' declared Robyn, somewhat aggressively. 'And now, I think you ought to go and help Janet organise some lunch. Your grandfather wants me to go over the production figures with him before Monday and, as you and I are going shopping in Sheffield this afternoon, now would seem as good a time as any.'

However, during the next week, Robyn couldn't help the illogical pleasure she got from the suspicion that Jared would not approve of her friendship with Mark Kingsley. Even Ben raised his eyebrows at the news that she was having dinner with Mark for the second time in four days, and although he didn't say anything his attitude spoke volumes.

For her part, Robyn was enjoying herself. Aside from the niggling awareness of Daniel's disapproval, she looked forward to her outings with the curate, and Mark's admiration did wonders for her self-esteem. For years, she had regarded herself as a woman approaching middle age, with nothing to look forward to but Daniel's future. To suddenly find herself the object of an attractive man's attentions restored a small measure of confidence to her, and she found herself looking in shop windows when she and Daniel went into town, studying current fashions in a way she hadn't done for ages.

There was no word from Jared, but Ben was not perturbed. 'He'll be back soon,' was his interpretation of his son's silence. 'Now that things are settled, there's not a lot to write about, is there? It couldn't have worked out better, could it? Imagine him making Daniel his heir! I never would have thought he had it in him.'

Robyn could have said that she had never actually endorsed the new arrangements, but she knew it wouldn't do her any good to make waves. Her compliance had been taken for granted and, until her own plans were finalised, it was easier to keep her own counsel. Besides, when it came to it, it was not going to be easy to thwart the old man. But in six months, Daniel would be old enough to go away to school, and when that happened, it would be a whole different situation.

In the meantime, she could quite see that her friendship with Mark could ease her position considerably. Not that she had any serious interest in him. She didn't. But she did enjoy being made to feel young and attractive again, and, in spite of Daniel's opposition, the plans for the pageant were gradually taking shape.

In the event, Daniel chose not to participate, and Robyn was not entirely convinced that Ben was not responsible. Her father-in-law seemed to take a delight in finding excuses why she shouldn't spend several evenings of the week at the church hall, and in consequence Daniel was often given permission to stay up for supper, just to keep his grandfather happy. It was a form of blackmail, and Robyn knew it, but with Christmas approaching she was inclined to be lenient. After all, if Daniel had been taking part in the pageant, he would have been up anyway, and it would be his birthday soon, and eight seemed considerably older than seven.

A week before the celebration, David McCloud's prediction of a white Christmas seemed to be coming true. It snowed hard áll day Tuesday, and when Robyn went out to get into her car to drive home from the mill, she almost lost her balance on the slippery surface of the yard.

'Don't worry,' she assured Joan Hedley, who had followed her down the steps, 'the main roads will be well salted. I just wish we had an indoor car park. It's going to take me fifteen minutes to clear the build-up from the windscreen.'

The road over Saddleford Tor was the most treacherous stretch of the journey, but the conditions had persuaded everyone to drive carefully, and she made it down into the valley without incident. Indeed, she felt quite pleased with herself for having braved the icy roads alone, and she was in no mood to listen to Ben when he argued that she should not go to the church hall that evening.

'If I can drive home from Ebbersley, I can drive the couple of miles into the village,' she exclaimed impatiently. 'Mark's only got a few days before the performance. I can't let him down when there's absolutely no reason why I shouldn't go.'

Ben sniffed. 'And is that all there is to it?' he asked, voicing his opinion for the first time, and Robyn frowned.

'All there is to what?' she enquired, deliberately misunderstanding him, and Ben regarded her dourly, his blue eyes remote.

'You're not telling me all this enthusiasm you're exhibiting is solely confined to amateur theatricals, are you?' her father-in-law demanded tersely. 'It seems to me, that young curate has more interest in you than he does in the pageant. Do I have to remind you that Stephen's not been dead six months yet? Do you want people to talk?'

Robyn caught her breath, stung by the unfairness of his remarks. 'Talk?' she echoed, controlling the sudden break in her voice. 'Do *I* want people to talk? I think that's a comment you might have offered to Stephen himself, or is there one law for women and another for men?'

Ben had the grace to colour, but he was not repentant. 'I know Stephen had his faults,' he declared. 'None better. But the lad's dead now. Can't we at least try and preserve his memory?'

Robyn's hands clenched. It was the first time in her life she could remember she and Ben having a conversation of this sort, and she realised with a pang that it was the first time she had really gone against his wishes.

'My—friendship, and that's all it is, whatever you think, with Mark Kingsley, in no way despoils my husband's memory,' she replied carefully. 'I cared for Stephen, and I'm sorry he's dead, but no one can pretend we had a normal marriage.'

'That's as may be.' Ben lifted one shoulder dismissingly. 'But don't imagine I'd countenance a *curate*——' and the way he said it was a scathing example of his frustration '—as a fit and proper person to bring up my grandson, because I wouldn't!'

Robyn was tempted to ask what he thought he could do about it, but old habits died hard, and she was loath to continue what was proving to be a most unpleasant conversation. Instead, she excused herself from the supper table and went up to her room to repair her make-up before going out, chafing at the realisation that Ben still thought he could control her life.

It was her own fault, she thought irritably, wiping away the smudge of mascara her shaking hand had left on her cheek. For so long, she had allowed herself to be controlled. In one respect, Jared had been right all those years ago. She had felt obliged to his father, and maybe that was why she had seen Stephen in a different light, instead of seeing for herself the kind of man he was.

Daniel was already in bed, and after saying goodnight to him she let herself out of the house without saying goodbye to her father-in-law. It was his own fault, she told herself grimly, wiping the latest layer of snow from her windscreen before opening the door of the estate car. He had to learn that Stephen's death had set her free in several different ways. Not least, it had given her the right to control her own, and Daniel's, lives, without the spectre of a custody battle should she and Stephen ever have split up.

Driving to the village was hazardous, particularly on the private road that bordered Saddlebridge itself. David McCloud had been out with the snow plough, clearing the roads around the estate, but further falls of snow and an ever-decreasing temperature had left the surfaces icy, and Robyn began to wonder if she hadn't been rather rash, after all.

Still, she refused to go back after what she had said, and Mark's welcome when she got to the church hall more than made up for any doubts she might be nurturing.

'What you need is a hot cup of coffee,' he said, pouring her one himself from the jug set on a Calor gas burner. 'There, that should warm you up. I wondered if you'd get here. It's been such a dreadful day.'

'Yes.' Looking round the sparsely populated hall, Robyn could quite see why he might have had his doubts. At least half the children hadn't turned up, and the chances of producing a realistic rehearsal tonight seemed very remote indeed.

'Well, we can always run through the script again,' declared Mark optimistically. 'Let's hope the snow is going to last. I've got high hopes for the pageant, and I know Mr Tomlinson is expecting a generous contribution from the proceeds for his charity for needy children.'

The rehearsal broke up soon after nine, with most people expressing the opinion that it would be wisest to get home before the roads froze over. Bidding the last group of parents goodbye, Mark gave Robyn a rueful smile, and when they were alone at last he pulled a wry face.

'So much for the dress rehearsal,' he said. 'I'll have to try and get everybody here on Thursday afternoon after school. We can't present the pageant without a proper rehearsal. Do you think you could possibly make it, about four o'clock?'

'I'll try,' promised Robyn, with a smile. 'Don't look so worried, Mark. It's not your fault the weather's turned so wintry. Besides, I can't remember the last white Christmas we had. It's quite romantic.'

'Romantic?'. Mark regarded her whimsically. 'Yes, I suppose it is romantic. It's still snowing, you know. How would you feel if we got snowed in?'

Robyn decided it would be wiser not to get involved in a discussion of that sort, and without answering him she reached for her tweed coat. She had bought the coat on her last trip into Sheffield, and she knew its longer length and tightly belted waist complimented her tall, slender figure. Since her involvement in the pageant, she had taken more interest in her appearance, and, although she knew she had Mark to thank for that, she had no wish for him to misinterpret their relationship any more than Ben.

'I think it's time I was leaving, too,' she said, after looping the strap of her bag over her shoulder. 'Ben will worry if I'm late, and after what happened to Stephen...'

'Of course.' Mark was always understanding. 'You will drive carefully, won't you? The roads out there are treacherous.'

'I'll be careful,' Robyn agreed gently. 'See you on Thursday, then. About four o'clock.'

'Until then,' nodded Mark, pulling open the door to allow her to step outside; but the sudden gust of snow that swept into the vestibule of the hall caused Robyn to take an unwary backward step. It brought her up against the solid barrier of Mark's cassock-clad body, and his arms circled her immediately, to save both Robyn and himself.

'I'm sorry,' she gasped, as he kicked the door shut again, and she was able to struggle free. 'It completely knocked me off balance. I hope I didn't hurt you. I'm not usually so clumsy.'

'You didn't hurt me at all,' Mark assured her, reaching out a hand to brush some flakes of snow from her shoulder. 'In fact,' his eyes searched her face, 'I quite enjoyed it. It's been something I've been wanting to do, but I haven't had the nerve until now.'

Robyn caught her breath. 'Oh, Mark——'

'I know. It's too soon after your husband's death. I realise that. But I just want you to know that when you're ready—well, I'll be here for you.'

Robyn shook her head. 'Mark——'

'Please.' He lifted a hand to silence her. 'Don't say anything more right now. Really, I do know about these things. It takes time. I know that. Just—remember I'm here when you feel able to—reciprocate.'

Robyn sighed. She wanted to tell him that, so far as she was concerned, Stephen's recent death had little to do with it, but she was afraid she might shock him. Besides, much as she liked him, she knew she was unlikely to fall in love with him. She was unlikely to fall in love with anybody, she acknowledged ruefully. That particular emotion seemed to have passed her by.

'Thanks,' she murmured at last, realising that until after the pageant it would be easier to leave things as they were. It was a shame, really. She had enjoyed his friendship. But, if Mark was looking for a more serious relationship, she would eventually have to tell him how she felt.

She opened the door herself this time, using the handle to brace herself against the blast of cold air that swept into the hallway. Then, bidding Mark goodnight, she marched determinedly through the snow to where the estate car awaited her. She would be glad to get home she thought. It was getting worse instead of better.

She swept the snow from the windscreen with her hand, shaking the wet flakes from her glove before unlocking the door and getting inside. The engine fired immediately, and she breathed a deep-felt sigh of relief.

Lifting one hand to wave at Mark, who was still standing in the church hall doorway, she put the vehicle into gear, and then offered a silent prayer as she released the clutch.

Instant traction sent the estate car crunching across the cobbled forecourt, and she applauded David Mc-Cloud's caution in renewing the tyres at the start of winter. So long as she could keep the car moving, she ought to make it easily, and the roads were so deserted that she was unlikely to encounter any obstacles.

She was turning into the estate when the accident happened. One minute, she had complete control of the vehicle, and the next, the wheels were sliding away from her towards the ditch that ran beneath the hedgerow. She had been in second gear, anyway, and she swiftly changed down in an effort to brake the car, but it was no good. Like a slow-motion replay, the heavy estate car slid sideways towards the hedge, tipping down into the ditch and lurching sickeningly to a halt.

Robyn wasn't hurt, just shocked; but the awareness of the damage to the estate car meant less at that moment than her own unhappy predicament. She was at least a mile and a half from the house—less over the paddock, but she couldn't risk that tonight—with no earthly way of contacting the McClouds, short of walking back to the village to find a phone. And, although the village might be perceptibly nearer, it didn't seem sensible to go back on her tracks, when her chances of reaching Saddlebridge were probably no more hazardous.

In the meantime it was continuing to snow and, realising that every minute she delayed was making her journey that much more difficult, Robyn switched off the ignition, and pushed to open her door.

A few seconds later, she abandoned that attempt, and scrambled across the passenger seat to open the other door. Her door was jammed tight against the side of the ditch, and she knew a little frisson of panic before the passenger door gave in to her feverish pressing.

It wasn't easy clambering out of the car, particularly as the door was heavy and she had to support its weight as she levered herself on to the side. But eventually she succeeded, albeit soaking her thighs and laddering her tights in the process. Allowing the door to slam again, she shuffled down on to the snowy bank.

It was a white world that confronted her, artificially illuminated by the snow. Familiar landmarks were obscured by the all-concealing blanket, and she felt a renewed sense of panic at the daunting walk ahead of her.

Keep calm, she told herself fiercely. She was reasonably equipped for the weather. Her tweed coat was very warm and, although her boots were more fashionable than practical, at least her feet were dry, which was something in her favour.

They weren't dry for long, however. Once she had assured herself that there was no way she could get the estate car out of the ditch again, and had started up the track towards the house, the snow soon seeped through the boots' thin soles. In a matter of minutes she was squelching in water, and her toes felt colder than she could have believed was possible.

Was it possible to get frostbite in the space of a few minutes? she wondered, thrusting her hands deep into the pockets of her coat, and wishing she could do the same with her feet. What if they went numb? Would she still be able to walk? What if she slipped and fell? Would anybody find her? And, if they did, would it be in time to save her?

She was panicking again, and although she kept telling herself that she had nothing to panic about she couldn't quite convince herself that it was true. She thought of Mark at the church hall, only a five-minute walk from the rectory, where he had warm rooms, cared for by Mrs Tomlinson, the vicar's wife. She thought of Ben, probably dozing by the library fire, still resentful of her determination to go against his wishes. And she reluctantly thought of Jared, no doubt sunning himself on some Australian beach, far away from the shivering chill of a typical British winter. Bondi Beach was near Sydney, wasn't it? That was probably where he was. Stretched out on golden sands, with some bikini-clad girl beside him, totally indifferent to her predicament, or her chances for survival.

Survival! Robyn expelled an impatient breath. Her position was not *that* desperate. She was cold and wet, and a little frightened, yes; but not facing a life-or-death situation. She would just be home considerably later than she had anticipated. With a bit of luck, no one would even notice she was missing. It was her own fault, after all, and the last thing she wanted was for Ben to start worrying.

Or was it? Wasn't she secretly hoping someone would start worrying about her? Oh, what she'd give for the sight of the Range Rover, ploughing its way towards her. Or David McCloud himself—another human being!

The sound of the car's engine, when it came to her ears, was partially obscured by the wind, whipping up the snow around her. Indeed, because it came from the opposite direction from which she had anticipated it, she was half inclined to believe it was some hallucinatory distortion of the wind itself. It wasn't until headlights swept the snow ahead of her that she turned to see the vehicle bearing down on her, and then she turned to wave her arms, weak with sudden relief.

Her relief was somewhat modified by the fact that the car was unfamiliar. No one she knew drove a dark-coloured sports saloon, and it wasn't until the car stopped beside her and the door was thrust open from inside that she realised who was driving.

'I—*Jared!*' she exclaimed, grasping the top of the door for support and gazing at him disbelievingly. 'But you—you didn't let us know you were coming back——'

'Get in, Robyn,' he commanded harshly, cutting in on her stammered consternation, and gesturing impatiently with his hand. 'If I stop here much longer, I shan't be able to move either. Do you want that, or do you want a ride home?'

Robyn hesitated only a moment before stumbling across the snow and climbing into the seat beside him.

Time enough to consider what Jared's unexpected return
might mean to her when she was warm again. Right now,
all she could think of was getting her feet out of their
freezing foot bath. Apologising automatically for covering the passenger seat with snow, and the carpet with
wet prints, she slumped beside him, letting him take the
strain of getting them back to the house.

Yet, in spite of her immediate needs, she couldn't help
a sidelong glance in his direction. Jared was back, she
acknowledged tensely, and this time it was for good. Her
futile hopes of having a normal Christmas at
Saddlebridge were melting as fast as the snowflakes
clinging to her sleeve. If only she felt more ready to face
him, she thought weakly, but once again he had taken
the initiative.

'Where have you been?' he asked, as he set the car in
motion again, and Robyn felt the warmth of his breath
against her cold cheeks.

'To—to the village,' she answered, equally as non-
committally, and she was conscious of him turning to
look at her again.

'To the village?' he echoed bleakly. 'What the hell
for?'

His anger was steadying, and she clung to it. 'You
don't have to swear,' she responded annoyingly. 'Is that
how you speak to women in Australia?'

'Don't bait me, Robyn,' he growled harshly. 'Just tell
me, who in their right minds would take a car out on
such a night?'

Robyn looked at him then, a deliberately insulting
stare. Even in the muted glow from the dash, she saw
the way his knuckles tightened over the wheel.

'It wasn't snowing like this in London,' he inserted
stiffly. 'And I should point out, it's not my car that's
wedged into the ditch at the gate.'

Robyn looked away from him then, watching the white
flakes driving into the windscreen. 'It wasn't snowing
like this when I went out, either,' she declared at last.
'And—and Mark was counting on me.'

'Mark?' She heard the sudden suspicion in his voice, and enjoyed her momentary advantage.

'Yes, Mark Kingsley,' she replied triumphantly, forgetting her physical discomforts for a brief spell. 'He's the new curate at St Peter's. He and I are—friends.'

She had been going to tell him about the pageant, but something, some malicious imp inside her, restrained her from making a full explanation. Let him think what he liked, she thought recklessly. The sooner he learned she had a life apart from the demands of the Morleys, the better.

What she was not prepared for was that her deliberately provoking words would cause him to put an unwary foot on the brake. With terrifying ease, the car went into a sideways skid and, although Jared fought with the wheel, the powerful saloon plunged helplessly into the mound of snow David McCloud had pushed to the side of the road. Its increasing momentum took it solidly into the frozen mountain and, although Jared spent several frustrating minutes trying to get traction on the rear wheels, they were too firmly embedded to move.

It was the last straw to Robyn, who had only just been feeling some return of sensation to her frozen fingers. 'You—you idiot!' she exclaimed, turning to him furiously and beating futilely at the arm nearest to her, still resting on the wheel. 'Don't you know you never brake on ice? Or have you spent so long in a hot climate, it's addled your brain?'

'It's not *my* brain that's addled!' he snarled angrily, lifting his arm so that her fists encountered the hard bone of his wrist. 'Cut that out, for Christ's sake! You're not exactly in a position to trade insults! If you hadn't gone out on some hare-brained date with a creep who ought to know better, I wouldn't have had to pick you up.'

'What do you mean by that? "A creep who ought to know better"?' stormed Robyn in return. 'Are you implying he would have to be a creep to want to go out with me?'

'I didn't say that,' muttered Jared impatiently. 'But, for Pete's sake, Steve's only been dead a little over two months, hasn't he? This Mark's a curate, you say. Doesn't that mean he's supposed to have some respect for the institution of marriage?'

'You—you hypocrite!' exclaimed Robyn incredulously. 'How dare you sit there and criticise Mark, when you have so much respect for the institution of marriage, you didn't think twice about making me your mistress!'

'My mistress!' Jared stared at her in the gloom, his green eyes glittering with sarcasm. 'My God, Robyn, all we did was spend an hour in bed together before you *were* married! That hardly constitutes a major affair!'

'It ruined my life!' retorted Robyn recklessly, and Jared's eyes narrowed.

'So Dan *is* my son,' he declared triumphantly.

'I didn't say that.'

'You didn't have to.' Jared shook his head. 'Well, well, well! Perhaps I'm not so sorry I rescued you after all.'

'This is a *rescue*?' Robyn demanded tremulously, unable to continue the argument in her present state of brittleness. 'How do you propose to get us out of here? Do you have a fork-lift truck hidden in the boot?'

Jared turned and stared out of the windscreen at the obvious disablement of the bonnet, hidden in the mound of snow. 'We'll have to walk,' he said flatly, turning back to her. 'I'm sorry, but there it is. There isn't any alternative.'

'So what's new? enquired Robyn, turning and thrusting open the door at her side of the car. Immediately, a gust of wind and snow swirled into the car, and she shivered. She had hoped to be home and safe, and in a hot bath by this time. As it was, she had at least another half-mile to cover in company with this objectionable man.

As she put her booted feet to the freezing surface of the snow again, Jared swung himself across the seat to join her. Then, hauling a leather jacket from the back of the car, he pulled it on over the sweater and suede jacket he was already wearing.

She set off without waiting for him, leaving him to lock up the car. It was all his fault; everything was his fault, she told herself uncharitably. If it hadn't been for him, she would probably not have got involved in Mark's attempts to organise the pageant; if she hadn't got involved in that, she would not have been driving in these conditions and at this hour of the evening. He was to blame. Jared was to blame. She couldn't wait to get away from him, and everything he stood for.

Even so, after traversing a hundred yards without hearing him catching up with her, she felt compelled to turn and look back. After all, he had rescued her, albeit temporarily, and her conscience wouldn't allow her to completely ignore his presence.

However, when she looked back, he wasn't there. He had disappeared. The expanse of snow she had crossed stretched emptily into the distance, and for an awful, heart-shuddering moment, she thought she had imagined the whole incident. She had heard of people doing things like that, particularly when they were in similar situations. Imagining they were safe and warm, when in reality they were freezing to death.

Her breath caught in her throat. Panic, which had been briefly conquered, rose like bile in the back of her throat. Dear God, she hadn't imagined Jared's return, had she? Surely, at a time like this, he was the last man she should be fantasising about.

Then she gulped. In her panic, she had taken a few steps back the way she had come, and now she could see again the dark mound of the car buried in the snow drift. So, she trembled with relief, no hallucination then, but where was he? Surely she hadn't missed her way, while he had gone and left her?

His sudden reappearance from around the other side of the car brought angry tears to her eyes. Had he been hiding? The sadistic bastard! Had he deliberately concealed himself to give her a mild heart attack? He had

almost succeeded, too, she acknowledged unsteadily. She
was so cold, she was easily confused, and she guessed
he knew her weakness and was deliberately playing on
it.

Swinging about again, she ignored his sudden shout,
and started back towards the house. Damn him! she
cursed bitterly, plunging on through the thickening storm
with eyes almost blinded by snow and self-pity. One day
she would get even with him; one day she would have
the last word. He would never know for sure if Daniel
was really his son. That was her secret. That would be
her vindication.

She was so intent on planning her revenge that she
was totally deaf to Jared's warning shouts behind her.
Besides, even if she had heard him, she doubted if she
would have paid any attention to him. So far as she was
concerned, at that moment Jared was all the monsters
in hell, and the devil incarnate, and any warning he might
be offering was bound to be a lie.

Consequently, her first intimation of the danger was
when Jared grabbed her from behind, jerking her backwards and tumbling her, and himself, into a pile of wet
snow. With the breath almost knocked out of her and
Jared's weight on top of her, Robyn could hardly mouth
the words of complaint that rose furiously inside her.
'How—how dare——' she got out thinly, gulping for
air, and Jared levered himself up on his elbows, to look
down into her pale, indignant face.

'The mere,' he said, breathless himself, and Robyn
felt the resistance seep out of her at his horrifying
explanation.

'No!' she said, even so, hardly daring to credit so awful
a solution.

He nodded. 'Yes,' he contradicted her tautly, his
breathing equally as shallow as hers. He slumped on to
her again, as the after-effects of what had so nearly happened swept over him. 'My God,' he muttered, his face
pressed into the hollow of her neck, 'I thought I wasn't
going to be able to catch you. If you'd walked into the

water, I doubt if either of us would have survived to tell the tale!'

'Oh, Jared,' she breathed, weakness overwhelming all else at that moment. Her hand came up and gripped the silky swathe of hair at the back of his neck. 'Jared, I'm sorry. I must have lost my bearings. With the snow covering everywhere, I completely forgot about the mere. Heavens, and it's swollen with all the snow we've been having! If I'd fallen in, you'd never have got me out.'

'I'd have had a bloody good try, or died in the attempt,' retorted Jared, lifting his face again. His green eyes raked her face in a penetrating appraisal. 'You crazy little bitch!' he added, with a return of impatience. 'I have no desire for Dan to inherit for a few more years yet.'

At the mention of her son's name, Robyn's fleeting sense of well-being dispersed. Whereas, moments before, she had scarcely been aware of the snow at her back, or the seeping wetness invading even her underwear, now its coldness penetrated even her skin. She was chilled, both inside and out, and common sense reminded her that just because Jared had saved her from drowning was no reason to believe he was any less determined to destroy her life.

'Let me get up,' she said, withdrawing her hand from his hair, and trying to push him away from her. But Jared seemed unwilling to be shifted.

'Not yet,' he said huskily, continuing to subject her to an unnerving scrutiny. With a growing sense of horror, she felt his cold hand against her cheek.

'Jared——'

'In a minute,' he insisted, allowing his hard knuckles to trail across the dry parchment of her lips. Then, when his thumb followed them, he pressed downward gently, parting her lips and pushing the pad of his thumb inside. He stroked it along the curve of her teeth until they felt as sensitised as the rest of her, and then slid his thumb between, to touch the involuntary participation of her tongue.

'So cold outside, and so warm within,' he murmured, and for a moment she was unable to answer him. 'You know, hearing my father talk about you, I half believed my memory had deceived me. But it hasn't, has it? Whatever the old man says about you being as dried up as an old maid isn't true. That's just his excuse for Steve making out with every available female in the district.'

Robyn gasped, shocked and hurt that her father-in-law should have spoken of her in that way. 'Ben—said that?' she choked, gazing up at Jared with disbelieving eyes, and then caught her breath instinctively as he suddenly bent his head.

His cold mouth touched hers gently at first, but then, feeling her involuntary withdrawal, he deepened the kiss. Pressing her back against the snow, he took possession of her mouth in a way that brooked no opposition, and the persuasive invasion of his tongue sent a heated warmth surging through her veins.

She had forgotten what it was like to be kissed by Jared. She had forgotten how helpless he made her feel, and how impossible it was to fight against him. It was crazy, she knew, and some sane corner of her mind stood back and mocked her foolish weakness, but she couldn't disguise her response to his touch. The coldness she had felt when Stephen had touched her, the downright revulsion she had experienced when Stephen had thrust himself upon her, and which she had come to believe was the legacy of what Jared had done to her, simply melted away beneath the searching hunger of Jared's mouth. The disturbing aggression of his tongue was no violation of her senses. It was a sensual reminder of the physical satisfaction they had once shared, and even through the thickness of their clothes she could feel his swelling arousal.

She was sinking into an imaginary haze of warmth and well-being, where all that mattered was that he should go on, drugging her with his mouth and crushing her beneath the hard pressure of his body, when Jared suddenly drew back from her. Immediately, the real awareness of how chilled she was swept over her, and without his broad protection she was once more exposed to the relentless fury of the storm.

'Come on. Get up,' he said, grasping her arm and hauling her to her feet with little regard for her finer sensitivities. 'If we're not careful, we're both going to die of exposure. Making love in a snowdrift may sound very romantic, but it's bloody cold in practice!'

Robyn pulled herself free of him, brushing snow from her sleeves and skirt with hands that were not quite steady. Would she have let him make love to her then, if he had wanted to? she asked herself incredulously. The answer was too emotive to even consider at the moment. The fact remained, she had let him kiss her, and responded. What price independence now, if he could undermine her will so easily?

'It's this way,' Jared directed, as she continued to avoid his gaze. 'Are you OK? Do you think you can make it? You wouldn't rather stay with the car, while I go for help?'

'No,' she mumbled at last, forcing her numb feet to move. The idea of staying in the comparatively warm car was appealing, but going with him seemed like a sort of penance for betraying herself and her son.

Refusing his offer of assistance, she trudged beside him up the track, following the line of heaped snow David McCloud had cleared earlier. Only dogged determination kept her going, forcing her to put one foot in front of the other over and over again, until the line of copper beeches that marked the beginning of the drive loomed familiarly before them.

'Not far now,' said Jared encouragingly. Chancing a look at him, Robyn saw his hair was white with snow. She probably looked worse than he did, she reflected dourly. Not exactly the image she had hoped to create for his return from Australia!

The sound of an approaching engine heralded David McCloud's arrival with the Range Rover. Seeing the two bedraggled hikers in his headlights, David swiftly brought the heavy vehicle to halt, leaning out to greet them with mild consternation.

'What's happened?' he exclaimed, and Jared gave him a wry look.

'Well, we didn't crash into each other, if that's what you're thinking,' he remarked, ignoring Robyn's instinctive withdrawal and propelling her grimly into the back of the Range Rover. 'But you might say we made similar mistakes,' he added, hauling himself into the seat beside the driver. 'For God's sake, turn this vehicle around and get us home. I'll tell you all the details when my extremities thaw out.'

CHAPTER EIGHT

HALF an hour later, Robyn was sitting in a deep, scented bath, sipping the hot toddy of whisky and water Janet had provided. She felt deliciously warm all over, the unpleasant side-effects of putting frozen limbs into heated water now having completely disappeared. She had washed her hair, too, and it was bound up now inside a heated towel, while the soapy suds of the water coated her emerging shoulders and arms in a concealing mantle of bubbles. She felt content—or almost. The memory of what had happened in the snow was still a painful reminder.

How had it happened? she asked herself impatiently, unable now to conceive how she had succumbed so easily to Jared's unprovoked assault. It wasn't as if the conditions had been conducive to a romantic interlude. She had been cold, and wet, and uncomfortable; and shocked, too, at the realisation of how close she had come to disaster. And yet, as soon as Jared had touched her, as soon as he had bent his head and stroked her helpless lips with his mouth, she had been vulnerable and, no matter how much she might despise herself, she had lost all awareness of her surroundings.

Perhaps the answer was that she had been in a state of ferment already. Perhaps the fact that she had had not one but three shocks in fairly swift succession accounted for her willingness to give in to his lovemaking. After all, she had to have been in something of a daze when she set off into the snow, or she would never have walked towards the mere. The little lake—it was scarcely more than a pond in dry weather—had been providing a haven for ducks and wild birds as long as she could remember, and she must have been confused to lose her bearings so completely.

Nevertheless, whatever the reasons behind her collapse, it *had* happened. For several significant minutes, she had allowed Jared to get beneath her guard and, although she might not care to admit it, if he had chosen to prolong the interlude she might not have been able to prevent it.

And he must know that, she thought uneasily. Just as he also knew that Daniel was his son. He had virtually forced her to admit it, and it would take all her ingenuity to regain the ground she'd lost. She knew better than to take his lovemaking on its face value. It was just another way to gain his own ends. He didn't care about her. He only cared about Daniel.

She shivered a little, in spite of the warmth of the bath, and when the door opened behind her she knew an overwhelming sense of relief to escape from her thoughts.

'Could you make me another one of these, Janet?' she asked, finishing the whisky and holding out her empty glass.

The glass was taken from her hand, but it was not Janet's comforting voice that broke into her reverie. 'I'll get you one myself in a few minutes,' said Jared smoothly, walking casually into her line of vision and looking down at her with a calculating green gaze. 'So— how do you feel now?'

'Will you get out of here?' exclaimed Robyn indignantly, sliding down into the bath so that the swelling curve of her breasts was concealed beneath the soapy water. 'Janet will be back at any moment, and what do you think she'll think if she finds you here?'

'I don't particularly care what Janet thinks——'

'Well, I do!' Robyn was incensed by his arrogance. 'What do you want, anyway? As you can see, I'm quite all right, thank you. If you'd asked Janet, she would have told you.'

'I prefer to see for myself,' declared Jared easily, making no attempt to leave. 'You know,' he tilted his head to one side, 'this is the first time I've seen you in the bath.'

'I should think so.' Robyn was astounded by this conversation. 'Jared——'

'We have to talk,' he said abruptly, setting down the glass and resting his hands alarmingly on the sides of the bath. 'Tonight.'

'I don't think——'

'I don't care what you think,' he said, his tone hardening. 'You've mucked me around long enough, and after what happened tonight——'

Robyn groaned inwardly. 'Yes. Yes—well, I wanted to talk to you about that,' she allowed after a pause. 'I mean——' She raised her eyes to his dark-skinned face and then swiftly lowered them again. 'I—I hope you didn't get the—the wrong impression.'

'Could I do that?' he countered softly, though there was no tenderness in his voice. 'As I recall it, you weren't exactly averse to what occurred.'

Robyn caught her breath. 'I was—startled. I didn't know what I was doing——'

'Like hell!'

'I didn't.' Robyn was compelled to look at him again, and her breathing quickened at the raw frustration burning in his eyes. All trace of compassion had disappeared, and they were facing one another as aggressively as they had done the night he had told his father his conditions for staying at Saddlebridge. 'I didn't!'

'Well, let's see, shall we?' he grated, and, before she realised his intentions, he had grasped her shoulders and hauled her up out of the water. Then, careless of what her wet, soapy body would do to the grey silk shirt and darker grey cord trousers he was wearing, he lifted her bodily into his arms and carried her into the adjoining bedroom.

'Let me go!' she exclaimed, struggling frantically to free herself, but the life Jared had led had more than prepared him to deal with a hysterical woman's protests, and all she succeeded in doing was drawing his attention to the exposed fullness of her breasts. Creamy-soft and pink-tipped from the bath, they brushed persistently against the front of his shirt, and he would not have been human if he had not been aware of it.

'Calm down,' he advised her thickly, his arm hard beneath the curve of her thighs. 'Or I'll think you want me to do something about it,' he added, and she immediately went limp.

'But this is ridiculous!' she whispered helplessly, as he deposited her with less care than a sack of potatoes in the middle of her bed. 'Jared, what do you think you're doing?'

'I should have thought that was obvious,' he retorted, crawling on to the bed beside her. He knelt over her, supporting himself with a hand at either side of her head. 'This is where we left off, isn't it?'

'No——'

'I think it is,' he insisted softly, but there was no warmth in his voice. On the contrary, she had the distinct impression that, in spite of his contention, he had only contempt for what he was doing.

Yet, when he bent his head to rub his cheek along the curve of her breast she couldn't deny the involuntary quiver that assailed her. Far from wanting to push him away, she had the almost irresistible urge to arch herself towards that tantalising caress, and when the slight roughness of his jaw grazed her nipple, she knew a shuddering ache of longing curl in the pit of her stomach.

Consequently, she didn't move when he drew one exploring finger down the dusky hollow between her breasts, and then continued on to her navel. With a tight hold on her emotions, she watched his cool gaze follow his enquiring finger, noticing his eyes linger longest on her breasts and on the inky black triangle of silky curls that marked the gateway to her womanhood.

'You know, if I were to judge from the clothes you wear and the way you behave, I could be forgiven for believing what Dad said,' he muttered with sudden impatience. 'But he doesn't know you as I know you, does he, Robyn? You're just as beautiful as I remember. And God knows, I've thought about you like this, ever since I went away.'

His words were briefly sobering, and she struggled to find the right way to appeal to him. 'Your father doesn't know anything!' she cried. 'Not from me, at least. I've kept your secret all these years. Why, in heaven's name, are you tormenting me now?'

But she had been wrong to talk of secrets. 'Yes,' he said, loosening the buttons of his wet shirt and tugging it out of his trousers. 'You're pretty good at keeping secrets, aren't you? But you betrayed yourself this evening, Robyn. For once I got you to tell the truth.'

'What—what truth?' she stammered, playing for time, while the sight of his lean brown body, gleaming in the lamplight, aroused all sorts of crazy thoughts inside her. His chest was muscled and smooth and only lightly traced with hair, the nipples standing so taught and erect that she longed to reach out and touch them.

'About Dan,' he reminded her tautly, tossing his shirt aside and lowering his chest to rub himself sensuously against her breasts. 'About my son,' he added, his voice muffled in the hollow of her neck. 'Go on, Robyn, tell me whose son he is now.'

'Jared...' With his tongue stroking the sensitive skin behind her ear, Robyn was finding it incredibly difficult to say anything and, giving in to a totally uncontrollable surge of feeling, her hands grasped the hair that curled at his nape, to drag his head up so that she could look into his face. His eyes were not calculating now, nor objective; they were glazed with emotion, and her own gaze fell before the fervent urgency of his.

'Do it,' he said, as if reading her thoughts. 'Kiss me, Robyn. You know you want to, and God help me! I want it, too.'

But still she hung back, and it was left to Jared, with a groan of impatience, to capture her face between his two hands and bring her quivering lips to his.

She clung to him then, her hands fastened round his wrists, as he delivered a series of open-mouthed caresses, that aroused but did not satisfy her. Each time his mouth left hers, she moaned in protest, and eventually she was compelled to release his wrists, and wind her arms around his neck.

Then it was Jared who took control. With sure, impatient fingers, he unwound the towel from her hair, so that its silken dampness tumbled about her shoulders in wanton abandon. Shifting back on his knees, he unbuttoned the waistband of his trousers and tore down the zip, turning on to his side to press the corduroy material down below his knees.

'Help me,' he commanded, dragging her trembling hands to his body. Hardly aware of what she was doing, acting purely on instinct, Robyn turned him on to his back beside her and buried her face in the flat hollow of his stomach.

'Christ, Robyn,' he muttered, kicking himself free of his trousers and reversing their positions. 'Don't you know better than that? How much do you think I can take?'

'I—thought you wanted me,' she breathed unsteadily, and with a groan of anguish Jared closed his eyes.

'I do want you, damn you!' he swore savagely, and parting her legs, he thrust himself into her. 'Too bloody much!' he muttered seconds later, and she felt his shuddering climax and the warmth of his seed inside her.

The sudden cessation of movement, without any conceivable advantage to her, was depressingly familiar. It might be years since Stephen had touched her, but the memory of her own inability to respond was as sharp as ever. She was incapable of feeling anything, she thought bleakly, and the fleeting belief she had had that it might be different this time was just so much wishful thinking.

A tear squeezed its way out of her tightly closed lids and trickled miserably down her cheek. The heated emotion of moments before had all dissipated, and all she felt now was shame and humiliation. It was all so horribly sordid, and she despised herself for allowing it to happen.

Her tear rolled inexorably towards Jared's shoulder, for he was slumped across her, and she was too late to prevent it from touching him. Instead, he felt its moist progress and, as it alerted him to her presence, he groaned.

'I'm sorry,' he grunted, levering himself up on his elbows, and Robyn turned her hot face aside from his belated pity.

'You had been warned,' she said bitterly, and with a muffled expletive Jared captured her chin in one hand and turned her face back to his.

'What do you mean?'

'What do you think I mean?' she countered, keeping her lids lowered. 'I'm sure your father told you. Stephen wouldn't keep that to himself.'

'What?' Jared was impatient. 'For Christ's sake, what are you talking about?'

'Don't pretend you don't know.' Robyn dragged her chin out of his hand. 'You've just proved it. I don't enjoy sex. I never have. Need I say more?'

Jared caught his breath. 'You're joking!'

'I wish I were.'

Jared shook his head. 'I don't believe it. Minutes ago, you were as hot as I was.'

'Minutes ago, yes.'

'Yes. And I blew it,' agreed Jared, staring angrily down at her. Then, comprehension causing a deep line to appear between his eyes, he gasped, 'Hey, you really don't know what you did, do you?'

'What *I* did?' Robyn looked at him then, and the dawning amusement in his eyes filled her with hot embarrassment. 'Why, you——'

But the hand she would have raised to rake his chest, he captured in his and brought to his lips, his tongue finding the sensitive centre of her palm. 'Oh, Robyn,' he said huskily, 'don't you know it was my fault that you didn't make it? I was to blame. I lost control. When you—well, when you touched me, I just lost my head. I'm sorry.'

Robin quivered. 'You don't understand. Stephen and I—that is, I never—I never have——'

'Never?' Jared's eyes narrowed. 'Except once, hmm?'

Robyn looked away from him again, her face burning. 'I don't remember.'

'Then perhaps I'd better remind you,' said Jared thickly, and when she would have twisted away from him he imprisoned her between his thighs and sought her trembling mouth once again.

This time, he invited her to touch him and, although at first Robyn was unwilling to do so, his hungry, demanding kisses soon brought her to the brink of the unknown territory she had so briefly glimpsed before. His stroking fingers took possession of her body, and with his hands finding every nerve, palpitating beneath her skin, and the warm male smell of him in her nostrils, it seemed the most natural thing in the world for her to reach for him, too. Her hands skittered from the sweat-moistened expanse of his chest to the thickening arc of hair that arrowed down below his narrow waist, finding the hard, muscled contours of his thighs overwhelmingly appealing.

'Gently,' he groaned, moving out of her grasp so that he could find the tantalising dip of her navel with his tongue. 'This is for you, not for me.'

'Is it?' she breathed, her hands tangling in his hair, pressing his face against her stomach. Jared uttered a muffled laugh.

'Well, maybe not entirely,' he breathed, his laughter disappearing as he sought her mouth once again. Then, with a trembling sense of apprehension, she felt him sliding inside her once again.

But, this time, it was different. This time, there was
no swift cessation of movement. This time, Jared
measured his length inside her in steady, even strokes,
so that in no time at all Robyn was moving with him,
matching her movements to his, and hearing the panting
sound of her own breathing echoing hollowly in her ears.

'Good?' he asked unsteadily, as her nails dug into the
skin of his shoulders, and she could only nod incoher-
ently. 'Just let it come,' he added, taking one of her
taut, swollen nipples in his mouth, and with a shuddering sensation that swept from her thighs through every
nerve and extremity of her body, she felt the miracle
happening. The incredible, unbelievable swells of
pleasure were sweeping over her in ever-increasing peaks,
lifting her, lifting her, higher and higher, until a sensation of total fulfilment enveloped her. She was hardly
aware of Jared's simultaneous release, or of the bone-
crushing weight of his satiated body on hers. She was
in a blissful lagoon of sensuous languor, with the barely
acknowledged awareness that he was responsible...

It was the sound of someone next door, in the bathroom,
letting the water out of the tub, that disturbed them.
And even then, Robyn was in too bemused a state to
fully appreciate what the sounds meant. But Jared must
have realised it was Janet, and with a swift, jack-knifing
movement he hauled himself off the bed and pulled on
his cord trousers. Robyn stirred protestingly as he swept
the quilt from under her and covered her with it, but,
by the time she had comprehended exactly what was
going on, Jared had picked up his shirt and was letting
himself out of the door.

It wasn't a moment too soon. As Robyn reluctantly
pushed herself up on her elbows, Janet came to the half-
open bedroom door, putting her head round the panels
to regard her mistress quizzically.

'Are you all right?'

Robyn felt the warm colour stain her cheeks. 'I—yes.
Shouldn't I be?'

'It's just that it's not like you to get into bed without drying your hair first,' remarked Janet drily. 'I wondered if you'd felt ill, or something.'

'Oh! No.' Robyn shook her head, aware as she did so of the wild tangle of her hair, loose about her shoulders. She put up a nervous hand and touched it experimentally. 'I did—dry it with the towel,' she murmured, unhappily, sure Janet would see through any excuses she might make. 'I was just—tired, I suppose.'

'Mmm.' Janet's expression was hard to read. 'Oh, well, so long as you're all right.' She grimaced. 'You know, you should wear your hair loose more often. With you living in this house with only an old man and a child for company, I sometimes forget you're still a young woman. But looking at you now—well, I'd say you looked younger than Jared.'

Robyn's face burned, but she was sure now that Janet's remarks were not as innocent as they appeared. Had the housekeeper seen her with Jared? Had she put her head round the door a few minutes earlier and seen them together? Robyn's pulses raced, and a sheen of sweat glazed her upper lip at the images that her mind created. Yet what would have been more natural but that Janet should check that she had finished in the bathroom, before letting the water out of the tub? And just now her sharp ears must have picked up the sound of Jared's departure, and that had enabled her to make her entrance with every appearance of confidence.

Robyn flopped back against her pillows and regarded the housekeeper doubtfully. 'You know, don't you?' she said unhappily, the excitement she had felt when Jared had made love to her rapidly disappearing. She felt empty suddenly, and not a little appalled at her own shameless behaviour. Maybe if Jared had still been there, she would not have felt so bad. But he had gone. He had done what he had come to do, and left her to face the consequences. What had been such a source of delight was rapidly turning into something sordid.

Janet was looking a little flustered now, and Robyn knew a moment's malicious satisfaction at someone else's embarrassment. Then decency reasserted itself and, tucking the quilt securely beneath her arms, she made a dismissing gesture.

'Don't answer that,' she murmured quickly. 'I—it's nothing to do with you, I know. Um—thank you for tidying up the bathroom. That—er—that whisky and water you brought me, it really was very welcome.'

Janet nodded, looking somewhat relieved. But then, as if Robyn's words had given her an opportunity to say something else, she hesitated. 'We—that is, David and I—we always had a soft spot for Jared, you know.'

Robyn expelled a weary breath. 'I know.'

'What I mean is—that's not to say we would condone anything he did.'

Robyn tried to smile. 'No?'

'No.' Janet caught her lower lip between her teeth. 'Look, Robyn, this may be none of my business——'

'I agree.'

'—but, well—if you and Jared were thinking of getting together, I couldn't be more pleased, and I know David——'

'We're not,' said Robyn baldly.

Janet blinked. 'You're not?'

'No.' There was an almost masochistic delight in shocking the other woman.

'I see.'

'I'm sorry.' Robyn's lips felt stiff and unnatural as she said the words. 'Naturally, I'm grateful that he was around tonight——' *and let her make what she liked of that!* '—but, as you inadvertently pointed out, Jared is a little young for me.'

'I didn't say that,' protested Janet forcefully, but Robyn had heard enough.

'I'm sorry,' she said again, turning on to her side and curling her arm beneath her head on the pillow. 'And I am—very tired. Do you mind?'

For a moment, she thought Janet was going to stand her ground and say something more, but presently she heard a muffled 'Goodnight' and the door between the bedroom and the bathroom closed with a distinct click.

'Goodnight,' Robyn echoed miserably, burying her face in the pillow, and the tears she had shed earlier were nothing compared to the storm of weeping that swept over her then.

CHAPTER NINE

ROBYN had a surprisingly good night, considering her state of mind. But the exhaustion of her walk in the storm—and the lingering lethargy of Jared's lovemaking—had combined to overwhelm her mental distraction. In consequence, she slept like a baby, and awoke with a feeling of well-being totally out of context in the prospect of the day facing her.

Nevertheless, she got up with a sense of purpose, determining not to allow Jared any advantage because of the previous night's events. She would show him she could take what had happened in her stride, and that, whatever his intentions had been, she was as resolute as ever that he should get no confirmation of Daniel's parentage from her. She had not forgotten his attitude towards her when he first came home from Australia, and she was no longer naïve enough as to imagine that, just because he had made love to her, he had any real liking for her. He was using her, that was all. He was determined to get concrete proof that he was Daniel's father, and until he did he was unscrupulous enough to use any means at his disposal to achieve his ends.

All the same, it was galling to remember how weak she had been. Their lovemaking might have been the spontaneous result of a series of events, but from Jared's point of view it could not have been more conveniently timed. He had caught her unprepared and unsuspecting, and because he had such a devastating effect on her senses, she had been unable to resist him.

Still, looking at what had happened more positively, it had proved she was not the sexual freak she had always thought herself. She did have feelings, normal feelings; she *could* respond. Maybe she was not entirely to blame

135

because Stephen had failed to arouse her. Maybe he had not been the right man for her. With someone else, someone like—well, Mark, for example, she might feel completely different.

She was cleaning her teeth when she heard someone in her bedroom, and her heart skipped a beat for a moment before she heard Daniel's tentative, 'Mum? Mum, are you in there?'

Immediately, she rinsed her teeth and grabbed for a towel, blotting her mouth as she opened the bathroom door. 'Hi,' she said, stepping into the bedroom and giving her son a warm smile. 'How are you this morning?'

'I shan't be able to go to school again,' announced Daniel, by way of an answer, and Robyn automatically moved to the window and swept the curtains aside. She had been so engrossed in her personal problems, she hadn't given a thought to the weather, but now she looked out on a snow-covered world, brilliantly white beneath a blue sky.

'Mr McCloud says it will take at least until lunch time to get the roads cleared,' Daniel added, joining her at the window. 'Can I go out and build a snowman, Mum? The forecast says the cold weather isn't going to last, and I'd really like to make one before the snow melts.'

Robyn ruffled his hair. 'I suppose so,' she said, noticing he had already dressed in jeans and a wool sweater. 'You look as if you had already anticipated my answer. No school uniform, hmm?'

'Well . . .' Daniel had the grace to look slightly shame-faced. 'Uncle Jared said he was sure you wouldn't mind.'

The muscles in Robyn's face stiffened. 'Uncle Jared?' she echoed bleakly, and Daniel groaned.

'You're not going to be mad at Uncle Jared again, are you, Mum?' he pleaded. 'According to Janet, he——'

'Mrs McCloud,' corrected Robyn automatically, and her son sighed.

'OK. According to Mrs McCloud, then,' he said exaggeratedly, 'Uncle Jared practically saved your life last night.' His eyes gleamed. 'Is that right, Mum? Did he really pull you out of a snow drift? Jan—I mean, Mrs McCloud said you crashed the estate car, and you had to walk nearly all the way from the village.'

'Mrs McCloud exaggerates, too,' retorted Robyn irritably, leaving the window to rummage through her drawers for some clean underwear. 'I didn't crash the car; it just skidded into a ditch. And I was only about a mile from home when it happened.'

'But Uncle Jared did rescue you, didn't he?' Daniel persisted, and Robyn lifted her head impatiently to look at him.

'He picked me up in his car, yes,' she agreed levelly. 'And then he ran his car off the road, too. I'd say it was arguable who saved who. You can tell your Uncle Jared that, next time he starts bragging about his heroics!'

'But it wasn't Uncle Jared who told me,' protested Daniel, staring at her frustratedly. 'I've told you. It was Janet—oh, Mrs McCloud!'

'And who told her?' enquired Robyn tautly. 'Your Uncle Jared, of course.'

'No, it wasn't.' Daniel was determined to defend his hero at all costs. 'It was Mr McCloud, actually. He said you must have almost walked into the mere. He's been out already, with the snow plough, you see, and he said you were lucky to be alive. He found your scarf—you know, the one you were wearing when you went out last night—sticking out of a pile of snow near the lake. He said you must have fallen into it, and that Uncle Jared must have pulled you out.'

Robyn's lips tightened. It was too near the truth for her to want to argue, but that didn't stop her from feeling irritated that Jared should once again have glorified himself in her son's eyes.

'And what did Uncle Jared say to that?' she asked, curious in spite of herself, but Daniel only shook his head.

'He wasn't there,' he declared carelessly. 'He didn't come down until later.' And then, as if he had only just noticed her appearance, he let out a whooping yell. 'Hey, Mum! What did you do to your hair last night? Did the snow get at it or something? You look like you went in for one of those Afro cuts, honestly!' He grinned. 'I like it. It's really neat.'

Robyn, who had scarcely glanced at her reflection this morning, for fear of what she might see, now took a good look at herself in the mirror. Daniel's idea of what was or was not 'neat' was not hers, and she gazed, appalled, at the sight that confronted her. Generally, she either secured her hair in a hairnet or plaited it in a braid to go to bed, but last night it had been barely dry when she lay down to sleep, and this morning the result of that was, unfortunately, plainly evident. She looked, as the old saying went, as if she had been dragged through a hedge backwards, and in spite of the colour in her cheeks, she thought she looked more like a witch than ever.

'My God!' she exclaimed, putting up a hand to touch the tangle of black hair that rioted round her head. 'I look like nothing on earth, Daniel! How can you even suggest that it looks *neat*?'

'Well—it looks all right,' protested Daniel defensively. 'It makes you look—nicer, *younger.*'

'Really?' Robyn wondered if a conspiracy had been formed to annoy her. 'Well, as soon as I can get a brush through it, I intend to wear it the way I always do. I am not a teenager, Daniel, I'm your mother! I have no intention of going around looking like some university drop-out!'

'What's a university drop-out?' enquired Daniel, frowning, but Robyn was in no mood now to satisfy him.

'Let's hope you never find out, hmm?' she suggested, urging him towards the door. 'Go along now, make your snowman, if you must. I want to get dressed.'

'But you're not going to work today, are you?' Daniel persisted, as he reached the doorway. 'Grandpa says that Saddleford Tor will be really dangerous. Perhaps you could come and make a snowman, too.'

'Perhaps,' said Robyn, non-committally, thinking that if Jared was involved, she'd rather not be. And yet, wouldn't staying out of his way convince him that she was afraid to face him again? And, while that might be true, she couldn't allow him to know it.

'Oh, great!' Daniel exclaimed delightedly, charging off along the corridor with his usual disregard for property, and Robyn closed her door. Oh, to be as young and ir-responsible as that again, she thought wistfully, leaning back against the panels. Had she ever been that young? she pondered. These days, it was difficult to believe so.

By the time she had brushed her hair and restored it to order, and dressed in one of her business outfits of hound's-tooth check skirt and beige wool sweater, she felt more equipped to face the day. Her smooth com-plexion revealed none of the anxious thoughts that still plagued her mind, and as she descended the stairs she was almost convinced that nothing Jared said, or did, could upset her.

The table in the morning-room was still laid for breakfast, with a half-full jug of orange juice sharing the honours with a pot of coffee, keeping warm over a low flame. But although Robyn could see her son through the window, making his snowman in the garden, there was no sign of her adversary, either at the breakfast table or outside. After helping herself to a cup of coffee, Robyn carried it through to the library.

As she had expected, her father-in-law was already in his position by the fire. Although, immediately after his stroke, Ben had had a full-time nurse to take care of him, these days he managed to look after himself with the help of the McClouds, grumbling about the regular health visitor, who insisted on keeping an eye on his progress.

Robyn half expected Jared to be with his father, and her frown mirrored her confusion that he was not. 'Um—good morning,' she murmured, allowing her tense nerves to relax once again. 'I—er—isn't Jared here? I—well, I thought he would be.'

'Telling me what a fool you made of yourself last night?' suggested Ben drily, looking up from the newspaper he was reading. 'I warned you about going out, but you wouldn't listen to me.'

Robyn sighed. 'It could have happened to anyone——'

'It *needn't* have happened to you,' retorted Ben, folding the paper and putting it aside. 'Do you realise, if Jared hadn't had the foresight to ring McCloud from London, no one might have noticed you were missing until it was too late? You didn't even come and say you were leaving.'

'Do you blame me?' Robyn walked to the window, and stared out at the snow. 'Anyway, you obviously know all about it. I'm sorry if I upset you. But you can't run my life for me, Ben. I have to make my own mistakes.'

'So you admit that it was a mistake, then? Going out with Kingsley, I mean?'

'No.' Robyn turned, coffee-cup raised to her lips. 'And I didn't go out with Mark, as you know. I just went to the rehearsal at the church hall, that's all.'

Ben grunted. 'You're not thinking of getting involved with him, then?'

Robyn gasped. 'That's my affair!'

'It's mine, too. And Jared's.'

'Jared's?' Robyn swallowed, stiffening. 'Do you mind explaining that?'

'Well, naturally it's of some concern to him if you're thinking of giving Daniel a stepfather. After all, if he's to make the boy his heir, he doesn't want some prissy curate filling Daniel's head with his ideas of how the mill should be run.'

'Oh! Oh, I see.' Robyn struggled to sustain her anger, but it wasn't easy when relief that Jared had not apparently betrayed her to his father was overwhelming all other emotions. 'Well, if—and I say *if*—that time ever comes, I'll be sure and let you both know well in advance,' she declared huskily. 'So,' she lifted her shoulders with the appearance of confidence, 'where is he?'

'Who? Jared?' She knew he knew exactly who she meant, and she remained silent. 'Well,' Ben was enjoying his moment of power, 'where else would he be on his first morning back? He's gone to the mill, of course. Where you'd be, I dare say, if you'd still been nominally in charge.'

The 'nominally' hurt, but Robyn ignored it. 'Do I take it my services there are no longer required?' she asked steadily, and Ben looked a little ashamed.

'No,' he said irritably. 'No, I should think Jared would be glad of your participation until the New Year, at least. But—well, you might as well know, Woodhouse has found some discrepancy in the figures. It looks as if—someone's been systematically defrauding the company, and Jared knows he's going to have to sort it all out.'

Robyn caught her breath. 'When did you find out?'

'As soon as Jared took charge. Old Maurice couldn't wait to tell him. Apparently, he'd mentioned the matter to you, but you'd just put him off.'

Robyn's jaw sagged. 'He didn't——'

'Well, anyway, Jared will get things straight.' Ben sighed. 'Don't look like that, Robyn. No one's accusing you. And you couldn't be expected to notice anything was wrong. You're not an accountant, are you?'

Robyn stared at him. 'What—what exactly did Maurice Woodhouse say?' she demanded.

'I don't know.' Ben was clearly unwilling to get into a discussion about it. 'For heaven's sake, Robyn, it's probably something and nothing! You know what old Maurice is like. He always did exaggerate.'

Robyn's lips trembled. But it wasn't with trepidation, it was with anger. *She* should have warned Jared of what she had found. She should have spoken to him before Maurice Woodhouse had the chance to enhance his reputation. Instead of imagining she had been the only person capable of detecting the discrepancies, she should have brought the matter up with Woodhouse himself.

Maybe he would have had more respect for her if he had known she had noticed the errors. As it was, he probably thought she was too stupid to read figures, and he had told Jared he had spoken to her to cover his own lack of confidence in her.

'Anyway,' continued Ben placatingly, 'I suppose you could hardly be expected to go in to the office today. McCloud says the front suspension of your car may be damaged. He's going to tow it into the garage as soon as the roads are cleared. It's best to have it examined; just in case there's anything wrong.'

Robyn pressed her now-empty cup between her palms. 'So how am I supposed to get about in the meantime?' she enquired in a tight voice.

'Well, you could always get a lift with Jared,' suggested Ben tentatively. 'It will only be for a few days, I should imagine. Unless you think he can manage without you.'

Robyn's nostrils flared. 'Is that what you think?'

Her father-in-law sighed. 'I think you're getting emotional, Robyn,' he declared, his agitated massage of the arm of his chair exhibiting his own tension. 'Would you ask Janet to get me some more coffee? I think this conversation has gone far enough.'

Robyn was tempted to ask him how she could be getting emotional when, according to what he had told Jared, she was just a dried-up old stick; but she thought better of it. Ben was a sick old man, after all, whatever his faults might be. And it wasn't anything to do with him that she felt so damnably helpless.

A slow thaw set in during the afternoon, and Janet informed Robyn that David had managed to pull her car out of the ditch and tow it into the garage in the village. With a bit of luck, there would be nothing seriously wrong with it, she thought, contenting herself with doing the household accounts, and writing some letters she had been putting off. The last thing she wanted was to have to ride to work with Jared, but until this matter of the company accounts was settled she knew that, whatever Ben said, she couldn't abandon her responsibilities.

Daniel had a fine day playing in the snow and, when he could eventually be persuaded to come indoors, he had a glowing, healthy colour. 'You should have come out, too, Mum,' he said, tucking into the plate of sandwiches Janet had provided for afternoon tea. 'Honestly, Grandpa, it was really great! And Mr McCloud says there could be some more snow tomorrow.'

'That's not what I heard,' said Robyn tolerantly, watching her son to avoid looking at her father-in-law. Although they had patched up their relationship at lunch time, she couldn't forget what had been said that morning. It was as she had feared, from the minute she learned that Jared was coming home. Nothing was ever going to be the same again. And, in spite of her resentment towards Jared for instigating those doubts, she couldn't help wondering if her position in this house had simply been a figment of her imagination.

The sound of the doorbell was a vaguely welcome distraction. Perhaps it was the garage, delivering her car, Robyn thought hopefully, looking towards the door. But, when Janet came to announce the visitor, it was not Sam Pearson who was waiting in the hall. 'It's Mr Kingsley, Robyn,' she said, glancing awkwardly over her shoulder. 'Shall I show him into the morning-room? I've not had the radiators on in the sitting-room.'

Before Robyn could speak, however, Ben intervened. 'No, show Mr Kingsley in here, Janet,' he exclaimed, twisting round in his chair. 'And fetch another cup. I expect the fellow won't say no to a cup of tea.'

Robyn got to her feet. 'Really, Ben, I——'

'What's the matter, Robyn? You're not ashamed of me, are you?' chided Ben ironically. Before she could denounce that thought, Mark came diffidently into the room.

'I say,' he said apologetically, 'if I've come at a difficult time——'

'Not a bit of it,' said Ben, gesturing with his good hand for Mark to take a seat. 'Daniel, offer Mr Kingsley a sandwich, there's a good chap. So, young man, how are you? Robyn tells me you're doing your best to put on a Christmas show.'

'A pageant, yes,' said Mark enthusiastically, evidently finding no difficulty in understanding what Ben had said. He took the seat he had been offered, but refused the sandwich a sulky Daniel unwillingly offered. 'With your daughter-in-law's help, of course,' he added gallantly. 'I don't think I could have managed without her valuable assistance.'

Robyn bent her head, refusing to acknowledge Mark's friendly salutation. She was still stunned by Ben's uncharacteristic show of cordiality. Usually, he avoided visitors like the plague, particularly well meaning ones, who were likely to sympathise with his condition.

'I'm sure Robyn's been a great help,' Ben was saying now, and Robyn could feel his eyes upon her. 'Of course, she hasn't been out much since Stephen's funeral. My son's death came as a terrible shock to all of us.'

'Of course.' Mark was suitably chastened, but the return of Janet with another cup and saucer and a fresh pot of tea rather spoiled the effect Ben was hoping to have, Robyn thought uncharitably.

'And how are you, sir?' Mark continued, when the housekeeper had departed, bringing a brief scowl of displeasure to the old man's features. Discussing his own health was not so amusing as using Mark to bait his daughter-in-law, and Robyn waited expectantly for the gruff dismissal she was sure was to come.

But to her surprise, Ben didn't respond in the way she had expected. 'Oh, I manage,' he said, adopting an air of pathos Robyn had never seen before. 'But, naturally, I rely on Robyn for companionship, and I have to say that, since she's become involved in this little production of yours, I've missed her. I really have.'

So that was it! Robyn stared at him resentfully. The old devil! He had invited Mark in, deliberately, to appeal to his sympathies. He was evidently not above doing that, if it meant he got his own way.

'But I understood your younger son was home,' Mark inserted now, and Robyn delightedly applauded his perception. She had expected Ben would have it all his own way, and it was reassuring to hear someone else defend her right to freedom.

However, Ben was not defeated so easily. 'Oh, Jared, you mean,' he said ruefully. 'Yes, he is home, as you say. But, unfortunately, since my elder son died, the mill has been left in rather inexperienced hands, and I think it's going to take Jared some time to put everything to rights.'

As Robyn seethed at this unwarranted criticism, Mark seemed to accept defeat. 'Oh, well, if Mrs Morley's absence is causing any trouble——'

'It's not,' put in Robyn flatly. Ignoring Ben's, and Daniel's, disapproving stares, she managed a smile. 'My father-in-law's only teasing you, Mark,' she added, flashing Ben a dare-to-contradict-me glance. 'If you only knew how independent he really is, you'd be amazed! And, as for needing my company—well, usually it's me who seeks him out.'

'Is that so?' Mark's relief was palpable, but Ben's hand had begun its familiar kneading of his chair arm. Maybe she was being mean in neglecting him, Robyn found herself worrying automatically. But then she remembered how Ben had disparaged her efforts at the mill, and hardened her heart. If she was ever going to make a life for herself, she had to start now. If she let the situation slide again, she might never find the strength to break away.

'Anyway, I really called to assure myself that you'd not suffered any ill effects from last night's little accident,' Mark added, surprising her once again. 'I met Mr Morley's chauffeur in Saddleford this morning,' he continued, explaining how he had come by that information. 'He said that you had had to walk some distance through the snow. I was appalled.'

'If you'd had anything about you, you wouldn't have allowed her to drive home alone,' retorted Ben, abandoning any further efforts to win sympathy, and Robyn sighed.

'Mark could hardly drive home with me,' she protested, and then broke off abruptly at the sound of voices in the hall outside.

'It's Uncle Jared! It's Uncle Jared!' exclaimed Daniel, his sullen expression leaving him as he ran towards the door. 'We're in here, Uncle Jared,' he yelled, jerking the door open, and Robyn met her father-in-law's amused gaze with unconcealed frustration.

Jared walked into the library without any self-consciousness, while Robyn had the utmost difficulty in even remaining where she was. She would have much preferred their first meeting since what had happened the night before to have been in private, but once again her wishes had to be subjugated to her brother-in-law's. It didn't help that in his dark three-piece suit and pale grey shirt he looked more attractive than ever; and the crisp bite of the wind had added colour to his dark face, extending his impact of healthy arrogance.

His eyes immediately sought Robyn's but, although she was aware of their appraisal, she refused to acknowledge them. In all honesty, she couldn't trust herself not to betray the painful embarrassment she was feeling, and instead she concentrated on Mark, trying to gauge his reaction to the other man.

'This is Mr Kingsley, from St Peter's,' said Ben at last, when it became obvious that Robyn was not about to make the introduction, and Jared's faintly quizzical expression lifted.

'Ah, yes, the new curate,' he remarked, and the way he said it made Robyn's blood boil. The trace of mild derision in his voice was not lost on her, even if Mark seemed to notice nothing amiss.

'That's right,' he said, getting politely to his feet to offer his hand. 'And you must be Robyn's brother-in-law, am I right?'

Robyn, chancing a glance in his direction, saw Jared's lips tighten. 'Jared Morley,' he agreed, taking the other man's hand with only a momentary hesitation. 'I understand you're the reason she drove into Saddleford yesterday evening. Wasn't that a rather foolhardy invitation, considering the conditions?'

Mark was taken aback, and Robyn had to bite her tongue to prevent the angry outburst that sprang to her lips at Jared's attack. How dared he? she asked herself incredulously. After what he did...

'As a matter of fact, I was surprised to see her myself,' Mark was saying now. 'So many people didn't turn up. It's a measure of her enthusiasm for the project that she was willing to take that chance...'

Jared frowned. 'The project?' he echoed. 'What project?'

'Oh, Mr Kingsley is trying to produce a Christmas pageant,' explained his father dismissively. 'You know, like Robyn produced herself some years ago. She's been helping him.'

'Has she?'

Jared's response was infuriatingly smug and, inadvertently meeting his gaze, Robyn had no doubts about what was going through his mind. He hadn't forgotten, any more than she had, that it was on the night of that other dress rehearsal that their relationship had changed so completely.

'Oh, yes,' Mark was going on now. 'It's been much easier with Robyn's assistance.'

'I bet it has.'

Jared acknowledged this with a mocking inclination of his head and, unable to prevent herself, Robyn intervened, 'As a matter of fact, we've helped each other,' she declared, standing up and aligning herself with Mark. 'Being with someone else—someone who didn't know Stephen—well, it's helped a lot. It's made me realise that life goes on.' She touched Mark's sleeve. 'I am grateful.'

'Oh—really——'

While Mark struggled to assure her that he had done nothing, nothing at all, Robyn enjoyed the unusual spectacle of Jared and Ben exchanging frustrated glances. And let them make what they liked of that, she thought maliciously. She was not an object, to be manipulated at will—even if past experience had led them to believe she was. She had a mind of her own, and it was high time she learned to use it.

However, when Daniel took the opportunity to claim Jared's attention for himself, Robyn's victory lost its bite. Moving away from Mark, she started gathering the dirty teacups on to the tray, and she wasn't surprised when Mark said he must be leaving.

'I'll see you out,' said Robyn at once, grateful for an excuse to get out of the room. And just for good measure, she added, 'Come along Daniel, you can get Mr Kingsley's coat.'

'Oh, Mum!'

Daniel's groan of protest was quickly stifled as his uncle pushed him gently but firmly in his mother's direction, with the promise that he would come and see his snowman later. Robyn quelled her own resentment at her brother-in-law's casual ability to restore her son's good humour, and took Daniel's hand firmly in hers. But it was frightening to see the power Jared had over the boy, and to anticipate what Daniel might do if he ever learned Jared was his natural father.

'I think you'd better abandon any thoughts of attending any more rehearsals until the weather improves, Robyn,' Mark observed, as he pulled on the warm overcoat Daniel had silently rescued from the closet. 'Besides, most of the work is done now, and with a bit of luck we may reach our target.'

'I'll come when I can,' replied Robyn firmly, despite Daniel's gloomy expression. 'I think we said tomorrow— at four o'clock, is that right?' She smiled at him enchantingly. 'I'll probably see you then.'

Mark took a step towards her, and then, remembering Daniel's presence, checked himself. 'Until tomorrow,' he agreed, his lips lifting with satisfaction. 'I shall look forward to it. And perhaps, afterwards, we might have dinner, hmm?'

'Perhaps,' said Robyn, belatedly remembering her reticence to give him the wrong impression. 'Perhaps,' she repeated, and consoled herself with the thought that she hadn't actually said yes.

'Why did you say you'd go to his silly rehearsal?' demanded Daniel, as soon as the door had closed behind the visitor. 'You know Grandpa won't like it, after what happened last night——'

'That will do, Daniel.' Robyn used her most quelling tone, her dark brows drawn together ominously. 'I suggest you leave me to manage my affairs and go upstairs and run your bath, before I remember you haven't been to school today and decide to give you some homework!'

'Mum!' Daniel was indignant. 'You know Uncle Jared promised we could go and see my snowman after Mr Kingsley had gone!'

'I doubt if Uncle Jared will be too distressed if you forget that promise,' retorted Robyn shortly, only to press her lips together in frustration as Jared himself emerged from the library.

'Ready, Dan?' he asked, infuriatingly, and the boy looked from one to the other of them in a pained demonstration of confusion.

'Oh, very well. Go and look at your snowman,' said Robyn tersely, taking pity on him. 'But I expect you to spend no more than fifteen minutes outside, do you hear me? It's dark and it's cold, and I don't want you going down with a cold for Christmas.'

'I'll see he doesn't,' said Jared, forcing her to look at him, though her eyes slid away from the challenge in his. 'By the way,' he added, as she turned towards the stairs, 'I'd like to talk to you later.' His lips twisted. 'Privately.'

Robyn stiffened. 'Very well.'

'Shall we say—after supper? In the study?'

'The study?' Robyn couldn't prevent the involuntary exclamation, and Jared inclined his head.

'It seems a suitable place to discuss business,' he averred, putting a familiar hand on Daniel's shoulder. 'So—come on, cobber. Let's go see this snowman.'

Robyn heard Daniel asking what 'cobber' meant as she went upstairs, as well as Jared's explanation that it was an Australian word meaning 'mate', but for once the casual affection in his voice didn't grate on her nerves. She was too involved with the prospect of what he intended to discuss with her later, and she thought how typical it was of him to startle her into divulging something incriminating, before revealing his own hand. He must know she had expected a discussion of a more intimate nature, but he had deliberately turned aside from the obvious conclusion.

Supper was a trial, so far as Robyn was concerned. She wasn't particularly hungry to begin with, and the awareness of what was to come after had affected what little appetite she had. Besides which, she had the beginnings of a headache, and the awful shivery feeling one developed immediately prior to going down with a cold. Of course, she thought impatiently, she would have to be the one to suffer for what had happened the night before. In more ways than one, she added, somewhat cynically. Having sex meant very little to a man, whereas she had never been able to regard it lightly. And, despite her determination not to let him get to her, she was unwillingly aware that he had. She had known that, the minute he had walked through the door that evening. Even furious with him as she was, she couldn't prevent the unwilling surge of heat that flooded her body every time she looked his way, and sitting opposite him at the table was the purest kind of mental torture. But, aside from everything else—the incongruousness of her infatuation for him, the difference in their ages—whatever he said, whatever he did, she must not forget that his real reason for coming to England in the first place had been to be near Daniel. It was Daniel he wanted, not her. Because of Daniel, she couldn't trust him. And without trust there was no future together, for any of them.

With thoughts like these for company, it was very difficult to concentrate on her meal, and she was inordinately relieved when it was over. She just wanted to get the upcoming interview done with, so that she could escape to bed, and she made no demur when Jared rose from the table and made their excuses to his father.

'I could remind you that it's still my company,' muttered Ben, when he heard what his son had to say. 'Anything you have to say to Robyn can be said in front of me.'

'I know that.' Jared had changed for dinner, and now he tucked his hands into the pockets of the dark brown suede jacket he was wearing. 'But I'd prefer to discuss this in private, if you don't mind. We don't want to embarrass Robyn, do we? Let me put her in the picture on my own.'

Robyn longed to wipe the complacent smile from his face, but she refrained from any overt retaliation. Instead, she contented herself with confining her resentment to a heated glare, wondering how she could be so stupid as to be attracted to him still.

With the door of Ben's study closed behind them, Jared lost no time in coming to the point. Robyn had barely crossed the floor to reach the desk, set squarely in the middle of the carpet, before his hands descended on her shoulders, hauling her back against him, and her stomach hollowed sickeningly as his mouth found the sensitive hollow below her ear.

'I've been wanting to do this ever since I got home,' he confessed huskily, his hands moving sensuously up and down her arms. His tongue searched for the nerves beneath her skin. 'My God, I'm shaking like a schoolboy! What a pity the door doesn't have a lock. I'd like to have you here, right now, just to prove a point, so to speak.'

Robyn was trembling, too, but somehow she managed to drag herself out of his arms and turned to face him with flushed cheeks and a cold-eyed dignity. 'You—you have a bloody nerve!' she choked, moistening her dry lips and avoiding looking at the unmistakable proof of his arousal. 'My God, indeed! And you said it was business! I wonder what your father would say if he could see you now!'

Jared stared at her furiously for several seconds, his eyes hot and undisguisedly savage. Then he looked away. Taking deep, steadying breaths, he directed his attention to the patterned whirls of the carpet, not trusting himself to lift his head until he was sure he was firmly in control again.

'All right,' he said, and she shrank away as he brushed past her, making for the desk with an obvious effort. Ignoring her involuntary withdrawal, he circled the desk to where a leather briefcase lay innocently on the pad. 'Business first,' he averred, flipping open the briefcase and extracting a file of papers. 'A matter of some two hundred thousand pounds, to be exact. The sum systematically withdrawn from the company assets over the past thirty months, and to which Maurice Woodhouse was allowed to draw my attention.'

CHAPTER TEN

ROBYN had to force her brain to start functioning again. 'Allowed?' she echoed stiffly. 'How—allowed? I'm sorry, but I don't think I understand what you're saying.'

'I'm sure you do.' Jared's eyes were cool and remote now, very different from the impassioned gaze he had subjected her to earlier. 'You did know there were some discrepancies in the figures, didn't you? In spite of what Woodhouse says, I can't believe even you could be that naïve!'

'Thank you.' Despite being strangled, Robyn's tone was taut with resentment.

'So—why did you let Woodhouse take the initiative? Why didn't you report the matter to me yourself? Surely it must have occurred to you that someone had to be responsible.'

'Have you overlooked the fact that you've been away?' Robyn exclaimed, struggling to compose herself, and Jared's mouth thinned.

'For two weeks only,' he informed her flatly. 'You had at least ten days to bring the matter to my attention before I left the country. I realise you still feel you have to protect Steve's memory, but for Christ's sake, did you have to give Maurice Woodhouse the chance to score?'

Robyn blinked. 'Maurice Woodhouse?'

Jared expelled his breath impatiently. 'You did discuss it with him, I assume?'

'No.'

'No?' Jared frowned. 'Are you sure?'

'Of course I'm sure.' Robyn sniffed. 'Look, what has Mr Woodhouse been saying? If he thinks he can blame me for——'

'Don't be silly,' Jared cut in shortly, giving her a be-littling look. Tossing the file on to the desk, he sprawled into his father's chair and regarded her frustratedly. 'No one's putting the finger on you. This has been going on for a lot longer than the three months you've been in the chair. In any case, you had no reason to do it. You haven't been running up debts at the bookmakers, have you?'

Robyn swallowed. 'Are—are you saying that—that Stephen did?'

Jared looked up at her through his lashes. 'Is that what you thought?'

'No.' Robyn was defensive. 'I—I hadn't come to any conclusion.'

'But it must have crossed your mind that Stephen was the most obvious candidate for suspicion,' said Jared thinly. 'Is that why you didn't tell me? Because you hoped I wouldn't find out?'

Robyn bent her head. 'I knew you'd find out—eventually. I—I would have told you——'

'But?'

'—I wanted to be sure, that's all.'

'And you didn't discuss it with Woodhouse?'

'No.'

'Why not?'

Robyn shrugged. 'He doesn't like me. He never accepted me as acting managing director. We never—talked. Not properly.'

Jared leaned forward suddenly, his arms along the arms of the chair, his hands resting on the rim of the desk. 'But he did consult you on fiscal matters? I mean, he would have to have your signature on any outlay of finance.'

'No.' Robyn squared her shoulders and looked at him. 'Your father left that responsibility to him.'

'Did he, by God?' Jared snorted disbelievingly. 'And no one expected I'd come back, least of all old man Woodhouse.'

Robyn said nothing. There was nothing she could say. It was obvious that Stephen was involved, and nothing she did now could prevent that from becoming public knowledge. She shivered. Even beyond the grave, it seemed, Stephen's reputation could still reach out to her and Daniel. She had hoped it could be avoided, but now Daniel was bound to learn his father had been a swindler, as well as a womaniser.

'I—I suppose there's no mistake?' she ventured, clinging desperately to that final straw, and she saw Jared force his attention back to her from whatever line of reasoning he was following.

'What? Oh, no, Stephen was involved all right,' he said, dashing any faint hope she may have had. 'I spoke to Manny Prince on the phone this afternoon. You do know who Manny Prince is, I suppose? You did know Stephen—occasionally made a bet?'

There was irony in his tone, and Robyn held up her head. Everyone had heard of Manny Prince's chain of betting shops. 'Does he—does Stephen still owe him some money, then?' she asked, holding on to her dignity, and Jared met her defensive gaze with weary resignation.

'I'd say that was the least of our worries, wouldn't you?' he declared, and Robyn had to steel herself not to give in to a totally futile surge of self-pity. 'But there may be a way to salvage something out of this mess. Tell me, are you sure Woodhouse never brought his suspicions to you?'

'I've said so, haven't I?' Robyn could see no way to salvage anything, and her throat felt tight. She was getting a cold, she thought miserably; as if she didn't have troubles enough already!

'What if I told you he says that you were always too busy to discuss the figures with him?' Jared volunteered suddenly, and Robyn blinked.

'Why would he say a thing like that?'

'That's what I'm wondering.'

She shook her head. 'Do you think he's trying to cover himself for not noticing what was going on?'

'He says he'd had his suspicions for some time.'

'Oh.' Robyn nodded. 'Well—he would, I suppose.'

'Hmm.' Jared frowned. 'I'm thinking that, too.'

Robyn made a helpless gesture. 'I wish he had said something to me. I might have been able to do something about it.'

'What?' Jared was sceptical.

'I don't know.' Robyn lifted her shoulders. 'Sold something, perhaps. I do have some jewellery, and there's a necklace my grandmother left me, which ought to be worth something.'

'Two hundred thousand pounds?' suggested Jared drily, and she flushed.

'All right. So it wouldn't have been enough. It might have been possible to arrange a loan——'

'Loans have to be paid back,' put in Jared cuttingly, and Robyn nails dug painfully into her palms.

'You're not very helpful!'

'And you're not very bright,' retorted Jared, with asperity. 'Don't you see? Hasn't it dawned on you yet? Woodhouse knows more about this than either you or I gave him credit for.' He lifted his hand and pressed the heel of his wrist against his forehead. 'Of course. That's why he brought his suspicions to me. He waited to see if you were going to say anything, and when you didn't he couldn't believe his luck. As soon as he heard I was coming back for good, he knew he had to do something. And who's going to suspect the man who points out the errors to you?'

'You mean—you think Stephen and he— together——'

She couldn't go on, and Jared nodded. 'It stands to reason, doesn't it? Look, Woodhouse is near to retiring age. Stephen had all kinds of monetary problems. And there's no one else likely to catch on to what they were doing. Not immediately, anyway. I guess Steve was always hoping for the big winner to solve his problems for him.'

Robyn stared at him. 'But—wouldn't he—Woodhouse, I mean—know that you'd guess what had been going on?'

'He might have. And then again, he might not. In any case, it was worth the gamble. What did he have to lose? As far as he was concerned, you knew nothing about it.'

Robyn was appalled. 'I can't believe it!'

'Why not?' Jared was laconic. 'This sort of thing goes on all the time, believe me.'

'And—and Stephen was—was swindling his own father.'

'I guess he'd argue it wasn't his father's company any longer.'

'But the shareholders!'

'Got smaller dividends. Times are hard. I suppose he thought they'd never notice.' He shrugged. 'Obviously, they didn't.'

Robyn's tongue circled her lips, and she frowned suddenly. 'What you said—about Mr Woodhouse believing I knew nothing about it—why did you think I did?'

'I found some calculations you'd been making in a drawer. I didn't know what they were at first, but, when old Woodhouse came with his tale of woe, I checked.'

Robyn pressed her lips together. 'I see.'

'It is my desk now, you know,' Jared reminded her gently. 'Don't look so dismayed. You don't want me to think you're involved in this, too, do you?'

Robyn gasped. 'I would never——' she began, her face blazing, and with a muffled imprecation, Jared got up and came round the desk towards her.

'And I'd never think it,' he exclaimed, catching her heaving shoulders and pulling her round to face him. 'For heaven's sake, Robyn, I'd trust you with my life, you know that. I've trusted you with my son's life all these years! Do you think I want to change that now?'

'I don't know what you want, do I?' Robyn cried frantically, struggling to be free of him before he overwhelmed her resistance yet again, and Jared swore angrily as her nail caught his unguarded cheek.

'You do know what I want,' he argued fiercely. 'I want you—and I want my son! It's what I've wanted ever since I was sixteen years old and you know it! So when are you going to stop fighting me and tell me what we both know to be the truth: that you want me, too?'

'I don't!' With an inhuman effort, Robyn tore herself away from him, putting the width of the floor between them as she rushed towards the door. 'I don't want anything to do with you, Jared, and I'll never let you take my son away from me. Just keep away from me, do you hear? Or Daniel and I will leave here, with or without your permission!'

Robyn would have liked nothing better than to pack her and Daniel's bags, and to get away from Saddlebridge for ever. Everything was getting much too much for her, and what had once been a sanctuary was fast becoming a prison.

But, whatever she might have liked to do, for the next few days, at least, she was compelled to abandon any thought of escape. The morning after that scene in Ben's study with Jared, she awakened with streaming eyes and a runny nose, and as soon as Janet saw her she ordered her back to bed.

'You don't want to infect everybody in the house before Christmas, now, do you?' she asked reasonably. 'Daniel can go to school, and I'm sure Jared is quite capable of running the mill without your help. You get back into bed. Dr Harrington is coming to see Mr Morley this morning, and I'll ask him to take a quick look at you, too.'

Robyn's protests that she didn't need a doctor fell on deaf ears, but she couldn't deny the feeling of relief she felt to be sliding back between the sheets. Maybe that was why she felt so defeated, she thought, seizing on that possibility as another bout of sneezing left her feeling weak. Colds could be quite exhausting, and she was sure she would feel better when her head stopped aching and her eyes stopped watering.

Daniel didn't come in to see her before he left for school. He simply shouted 'Goodbye' from outside, and she had to summon all her strength to answer him.

'Have a good day, darling,' she called huskily, wishing he was older and therefore less vulnerable. She dreaded to think what would be said at school when it came out that his father was an embezzler, as well as an unfaithful husband. She might even be asked to remove him. Adultery was one thing, fraud was another.

Dr Harrington came during the morning and pronounced she had a severe case of coryza. 'In other words, the common cold, young woman,' he remarked, folding his stethoscope back into his bag. 'Janet tells me you've been standing about in draughty church halls, without proper protection, and that a long evening walk in the snow has aggravated your condition.'

'She would,' said Robyn miserably, glad to pull the covers over herself again. 'I've just been helping the curate with his Christmas show, that's all. And my car broke down when I was on my way home.'

'A little bird told me you ran it into the ditch,' observed Dr Harrington, with the familiarity of a long association. 'Never mind. You'll survive,' he added humorously. 'I'll pop in and see you again at the weekend. You should be feeling much better by then.'

Robyn hoped so, although she wasn't optimistic. The way she felt right now, it didn't seem possible that she would ever feel better, and when her eyes streamed again there were tears mixed with the outflow.

Of course, there were some advantages to being confined to her room. It meant she was not expected to face any visitors for several days, and the dual problems of Stephen's dishonesty and Daniel's parentage could be temporarily set aside.

Eventually, she knew, she would have to face the damaging results of what her husband had done. There was no avoiding it, and in her lower moments she thought

how smug Jared must be feeling in the present situation.
That Stephen, who had always been his father's favourite and therefore above reproach, should have let him
down so badly, must be a bitter pill for Ben to swallow,
and she supposed it was only natural that Jared should
enjoy his vindication. Nevertheless, she was glad she
didn't have to be there to see it.

So far as Daniel was concerned, her feelings were
rather less unequivocal. On the one hand, she welcomed
the opportunity of a breathing space before having to
speak to Jared again, but on the other, when both Jared
and her son were in the house and therefore possibly
together, she fretted over what might be said between
them. She couldn't deny that what had happened on the
night of the storm had upset all her preconceived ideas
about a lot of things, but she still clung to the premise
that Jared was simply using her to gain his own ends.
Nothing he had done before or since had convinced her
there could be any other reason for his behaviour. Every
kiss, every caress, every intimate moment between them,
seemed to have been engineered to persuade her to
commit the ultimate folly of admitting the truth and, no
matter what he said, she couldn't believe he really wanted
her. He might have done once—but that was many years
ago. She was older now, *much* older.

One other outcome of her illness was that she was
obliged to abandon any hopes of continuing with the
church pageant. In spite of the fact that, on Thursday
afternoon, a steady thaw cleared most of the roads,
Robyn was forced to accept Janet's offer to telephone
Mark with the news.

'There's no way you're going to be fit enough to spend
several hours in that draughty old place,' the housekeeper asserted firmly, when Robyn ventured that she
might be well enough to attend Saturday evening's performance. 'He'll have to manage without you. Mr
Morley's adamant about that.'

'*Mr* Morley is?' Robyn was tempted to ask what Mr Morley had to do with it, but she was too worn out with sneezing and blowing her nose to start an argument.

'That's what I said,' declared Janet, not realising she was pushing her luck. 'So—how about a nice poached egg on toast, hmm? That won't take much eating, now, will it?'

Robyn made a weary gesture. 'I'm not really very hungry, Janet,' she murmured, feeling as if everything—her own body included—was combining to balk any plans she might have for asserting her independence. Even her friendship with Mark was being thwarted by circumstances totally beyond her control, and she felt completely helpless.

By Saturday, however, she had recovered a little of her strength. The worst effects of the head cold had left her, and only a harsh cough remained. She still felt weak, and a little heady after spending two full days in bed, but her brain was functioning again. She no longer had the muzzy sense of viewing herself from outside her body and, although to her own eyes she looked ghastly, Janet insisted she had a little more colour in her cheeks.

'Another couple of days and she'll be right as rain, don't you think, Doctor?' she suggested, when Dr Harrington returned on Saturday morning, and the elderly physician had to concede that she was right.

'Yes, two more days should make a world of difference,' he agreed, although his expression was curiously troubled as he met his patient's anxious gaze. 'And then perhaps you could come and see me at the surgery, Robyn,' he added, and Robyn knew a disturbing sense of foreboding at his unexpected invitation.

'There's nothing wrong, is there, Doctor?' exclaimed Janet at once, voicing Robyn's own fears. As if realising his words could be misconstrued, Dr Harrington attempted to reassure her.

'Nothing wrong, no,' he said, closing his bag and giving a hearty smile that was, nevertheless, forced. 'It's just a little matter I wanted to—discuss with you, Robyn,' he added, and as Janet showed him out, Robyn guessed exactly what that little matter must be. *Jared!* she thought sickly. It had to be something to do with Jared—and Daniel! For heaven's sake, had Jared voiced his suspicions to Dr Harrington? Was that why the doctor wanted to talk to her? To ask her about the premature delivery of a baby that had been born almost eight years ago?

It was a horrifying proposition, but Robyn could think of no alternative. But that Jared should do such a thing! She could hardly believe it. What must Dr Harrington be thinking? Oh, she had been so right not to trust Jared, *ever*.

When Janet came back, Daniel was with her, and with her recent insight into Jared's character foremost in her mind, Robyn pulled her son towards her and gave him a fervent hug.

'Hey!' protested Janet, as Daniel struggled in some embarrassment to free himself. 'You're still contagious, Robyn. Let the boy go. He's not going to run away, are you, Daniel?'

Daniel grimaced, somewhat awkwardly, and settled himself on the foot of his mother's bed. Then, brushing a hand over his flushed cheeks, he muttered, 'How are you, Mum? Janet says you're feeling better.'

Robyn was going to reprove him for using the housekeeper's Christian name, but somehow it was too much of an effort. Instead, she assured him she was feeling much better, and then, in a guarded voice, she added, 'And where's your uncle this morning?'

'Uncle Jared?' exclaimed Daniel in some surprise, and Robyn bit back the obvious rejoinder. 'Oh, he's downstairs. D'you want to see him?'

'No.' Robyn gave Janet an awkward smile. 'I—just wondered, that's all.'

'I expect both he and Mr Morley will be glad to see you up and about again,' remarked the housekeeper severely. She was not unaware of the antipathy that existed between her mistress and her employer's younger son, and this was her way of letting Robyn know she didn't endorse it. 'But now, young man, you'd better ask your mother what you came to ask her, and then we'll go and let her get some rest.'

'Oh! Oh, yes.' Daniel looked somewhat discomfited now, and Robyn gazed at him with sudden anxiety.

'What is it?' she asked. 'What do you want to ask me?'

Daniel looked at Janet, then at his mother, and then down at his hands, clenching over the knees of his jeans. 'Um, well—would you mind if I went Christmas shopping with Uncle Jared?' he mumbled awkwardly. And then, with more confidence, 'He says he'll take me into Sheffield.' He lifted his head, his eyes shining. 'Can I go, Mum? Please?'

Robyn's eyes moved to the housekeeper's now, too, and Janet gave a little dismissing shake of her shoulders. It was obvious she saw nothing out of the ordinary in Daniel's request, and Robyn knew an overpowering feeling of frustration at her own helplessness.

'I—well——' Avoiding Janet's gaze now, Robyn shifted uneasily. 'I'll take you into Sheffield on Monday. Now that you've finished school, we can go whenever we like. It'll be Christmas Eve on Tuesday. We could go then.'

'I think it's highly unlikely you'll be going anywhere before Christmas,' put in Janet flatly. 'For heaven's sake, Robyn, you're not going to be strong enough to trail around Sheffield shopping. Let him go with his uncle. Jared will enjoy it, and so will he.'

Robyn had no doubt about that, but she dared not allow it. After what Dr Harrington had said, how could she trust Jared not to betray his suspicions to her son?

'I'm sorry,' she said now, and Daniel gave a cry of dismay. 'It's no use, Daniel. My mind is made up. In any case, Uncle Jared has—has more important things to do than take you shopp——'

'No, he doesn't.'

The quiet rejoinder came from the doorway and, turning her head, Robyn was infuriated to see Jared standing in the opening, watching them. Then, without waiting for an invitation, he walked casually into the room, smiling reassuringly at Daniel and exchanging an understanding glance with Janet.

But when he came to the bed, his smile disappeared. 'So,' he said, pushing his hands into the pockets of the brown cord jacket he was wearing, 'I understand you're feeling better. Perhaps you'll be fit enough to get up this afternoon, hmm? I won't be here, but I know my father would like to see you.'

Was that a warning? Or a threat? Looking up into Jared's enigmatic face, Robyn couldn't be sure. But it had brought the memory of Stephen's dishonesty sharply back into focus, and she guessed that had been his intention.

'I—may get up,' she ventured tightly, irritably aware that it mattered to her that he was seeing her at her worst. It wasn't important, she told herself fiercely, resisting the urge to touch her braid or check that the buttons of her nightshirt were securely fastened. But the trouble was, it *was* important, and she despised the treacherous emotions that fed such an unworthy weakness.

'And you are feeling better?' he prompted, as Daniel got up and came to stand beside him. 'Dr Harrington says you've been lucky. It could have turned to pneumonia.'

'Aren't I the lucky one!' Robyn's lips were tight. 'But now, if you don't mind——'

'But what about Sheffield?' protested Daniel, clearly not prepared to give up now he had an ally. But, before Robyn could repeat what she had said before, Jared put a warning hand on her son's shoulder.

'Let me talk to your mother, Dan,' he said, pushing the boy gently towards the housekeeper. 'You go downstairs with Janet. I'll be with you in a minute.'

Robyn wanted to protest, too, but she was loath to create a scene in front of Daniel. Besides, Janet, too, was all ears, and there were things she wanted to say to Jared which were not fit for anyone else to hear.

The door closed behind the others a few moments later, and Robyn wished she could have conducted this conversation anywhere else than in her bed. As if Jared didn't have advantages enough, she brooded, aware of his dark-skinned strength and harsh good looks with every fibre of her being. He looked young and virile, while she felt pale, and unhealthy, and decidedly old. How could she hope to compete, when it came to Daniel's affections?

'Before you start, I should tell you that I know all about what you've been doing?' she burst out, before he could say anything. 'And—and I want you to know, I think you're disgusting! Disgusting, and—and contemptible!'

'Really?' Jared frowned. 'For inviting Dan to go to Sheffield with me?'

Robyn's lips curled. 'No! No, of course not. You—you know what I mean. How—how dare you stand there and pretend you don't?'

Jared took his hands out of his pockets and ran weary fingers through his hair. 'Well, I'm sorry, but you're going to have to enlighten me,' he said flatly. 'Are you talking about what happened the other night? Are you going to tell me that what happened was all a mistake? I guess, after what happened the last time, I should have expected——'

'Damn you, this has nothing to do with what happened the other night!' cried Robyn, fairly simmering with frustration. 'Oh, for heaven's sake, you can stop acting now. You don't have to pretend any more. Didn't it occur to you that Dr Harrington might say something to me? He's an old man, and an old friend; naturally, he must be wondering what's going on.'

Jared's brows arched. 'And what is?'

Robyn gasped. 'You tell me.'

Jared shrugged, and then, to her astonishment, he lowered his weight on to the side of the bed, the hard bone of his hip taut against her thigh. Then, ignoring her efforts to evade him, he took her left hand between both of his, and smoothed his thumb over the narrow band of her wedding ring.

There was a shocked silence as Robyn absorbed the fact that Jared was struggling with some emotion, too, and then she tugged her hand away, and thrust it under the covers. She was trembling, as much with her awareness of him as with any sense of confusion she might be feeling, and she wondered somewhat blankly what he expected her to say.

Taking a deep breath, she began again. 'Why did you go to see Dr Harrington?' she asked unsteadily. 'You might as well admit it. He's virtually said as much to me.'

'Has he?' Jared seemed unperturbed. 'And what did he say, exactly?'

'Well——' Robyn was annoyed to find she was on the defensive again. 'He said—he said he wants me to go and see him. At the surgery. As soon as I'm fit enough to go into the village.'

'And what has that got to do with me?' Jared was so reasonable, she wanted to scream.

'Don't pretend, Jared.'

'I'm not.'

'You're not denying you went to see him, I notice.'

'I—went to the surgery a couple of weeks ago, yes.'

'A couple of weeks—*why*?'

'He asked me to come in. We spoke about Dad. I asked him if there was any chance of him recovering sufficiently to go back to the mill.'

Robyn swallowed. 'And?'

'And he said no. But I'm sure you could have answered that yourself. I don't think it was such a contemptible thing to do. I wanted to know the score, before I severed all ties with Australia.'

Robyn stared at him. 'What else did you ask him?'

'What else?' Jared shook his head. 'Nothing else.'

'Liar!'

'Now, listen to me——' With a roughening of his voice, Jared leant towards her then, grasping her shoulders in a painful grip, and staring at her with tormented eyes. 'Suppose you tell me what all this is about, hmm? What am I supposed to have done? What could Dr Harrington tell me that I don't already know?'

Robyn trembled. 'You know!'

'About Dan?' Jared's lips twisted, and with a violent gesture he set her free. 'What do you think he could tell me, do you suppose? I hate to disillusion you, Robyn, but doctors can't prove conclusively who a child's father might be.'

Robyn blinked. 'They can't?'

'No, they can't.' Jared regarded her coldly. 'Did you really think I might ask Dr Harrington about something like that?'

Robyn swallowed. 'Well——'

'You did think it, didn't you?' Jared's mouth tightened. 'My God! You must hate me, Robyn. I didn't want to believe it, but gradually you're convincing me.'

Robyn shook her head. 'I don't—hate you, Jared——'

'But you don't like me much, either,' muttered Jared harshly, getting abruptly up from the bed. 'But don't worry, Robyn. I've finally got the message. Anything I thought there was between us all those years ago—it's over. I'm through with trying to persuade you that we could still have a life together. You've got your memories, such as they are, and you've got your son! That's all you ever wanted, only I was too stubborn to realise it before.'

Robyn looked up at him. 'And—and you won't—you won't tell Daniel?' she ventured unsteadily.

'Tell him?' Jared was bleak. 'Tell him what?'

'Oh, please...' Robyn knew she was pleading with him, but she couldn't help it. 'You're not—you're not going to tell him who his father really is, are you? I—I'll do anything you say, just don't tell him the truth.'

If anything, Jared looked even colder. 'I doubt if you'd recognise the truth if you heard it,' he said savagely. 'In any case, I don't have to tell Dan anything about his father. He knows.'

'He knows!' Robyn's face grew even paler than it already was. 'How—how does he know? Have you already told him?'

Jared swore. 'I didn't have to tell him,' he declared harshly, and then, at her gulp of despair, he added, 'He's always known, Robyn. Stephen *was* his father. Believe me, I know what I'm talking about. If you'd made a few simple enquiries yourself, you could have saved both of us a lot of anguish. What I said about doctors not being able to distinguish who a child's father might be is only half the story. Stephen and I had different mothers; we had different blood types. I'm sorry to disappoint you, but Dan isn't my son!'

Robyn was stunned. She couldn't believe it, after all these years, to learn she had been living a lie. It couldn't be true. Was Daniel really *Stephen's* son? Had he really been three weeks premature, and not the one week overdue that she had always assumed? Oh, how could she have been so stupid? How could she have been so naïve? Jared had *known*, yet, if she hadn't brought it up, he hadn't been going to tell her!

He was at the door when she found her tongue. 'How—how could you?' she choked. 'How could you let me go on believing—believing——'

'What?' Jared was contemptuous. 'That Dan was my son? You denied he was, remember?'

'But you knew——'

'No. I didn't *know* anything. I thought I did, but I didn't. Not until the other night, when you made me so mad. I decided to make some enquiries for myself. Oh—not from Harrington,' Jared added scornfully. 'Even I couldn't go that far. But I already knew Stephen's blood type, and my own, and the private maternity home in Sheffield still had the records they made when Daniel was born.'

CHAPTER ELEVEN

FOR the rest of the morning, Robyn felt numb. Even when Janet came to tell her that Jared had taken Daniel into Sheffield, she made no demur, and she guessed the housekeeper was curious at her apparent change of heart.

But she couldn't help it. For so long she had lived with the fear that someone else would find out Daniel was not Stephen's son, that now that fear had been removed she felt incapable of absorbing it. It was as if it was all a dream, as if she had imagined that scene with Jared, and soon she would wake up and find everything was as it was before. It wasn't possible that she had been mistaken. Daniel wasn't Stephen's son, he was Jared's.

At lunch time, Janet brought her tray, and the suggestion that she might get dressed and go downstairs afterwards. 'I know Mr Morley would like to see you,' she said. 'And you know it's impossible for him to come upstairs.'

Robyn gave a thin smile. 'I might do that,' she said, realising that was one problem that would not go away. Sooner or later, she had to talk to Ben about Stephen's embezzlement. It wasn't going to be easy, but no doubt Jared had told him what had been going on in his absence.

'You're all right, aren't you, Robyn?' Janet persisted, lingering even after her mistress had picked up her spoon and was making a brave effort to tackle the bowl of creamed soup she had brought her. 'I mean,' she added, when Robyn looked up at her a little warily, 'you don't really mind that Jared's taken Daniel into Sheffield, do you? I know Jared said you wouldn't, and you didn't object when I told you earlier, but—well, you seemed so—tense, somehow. I hope you're not worrying about the boy.'

Robyn expelled her breath on a sigh. 'No,' she said at last. 'No, I'm not worrying about Daniel.'

'But you are worrying about something else?' Janet was quick to notice the qualification.

'I—no.' Robyn knew that, however attractive the proposition might be, she could not discuss her present problems with Janet. 'But—er—thanks for your concern. I do appreciate it, honestly.'

Janet gave a rueful smile. 'Oh, well... So, I'll tell Mr Morley you'll be down later, shall I?'

Robyn hesitated a moment, and then she nodded. 'Why not?' she agreed flatly. 'I don't have anything else to do.'

Robyn took a shower and washed her hair before attempting to get dressed. It was a foolish notion, she knew, after all that had gone before, but she wanted to look her best the next time Jared saw her. There was not a lot she could do to mask the puffiness around her eyes, and the hollows in her cheeks were the result of more than just a few days' loss of appetite. Ever since Jared had come home, she had lived on the knife edge of her emotions, and it was no surprise that it was beginning to show. Nevertheless, she was determined to show him that his words had not devastated her, even if, deep inside her, the knowledge that Daniel was not Jared's child had been a shattering revelation.

But the real truth was, she was not relieved. Not really. After all this time, and all this soul-searching, she was only just beginning to understand her real feelings. She loved Jared. She knew that now. She probably always had. Only always, in the back of her mind, she had blamed him—and herself—for something that had never been their fault. Jared had not made her frigid with Stephen; Stephen had done that for himself. But until the guilt she had always felt about Daniel's conception had been removed, she had been unable to accept it.

Ben was in the library when she eventually went downstairs. With a rug across his knees, he was seated in his usual position beside the fire, and his eyes took on a grudging approval as his daughter-in-law came into the room.

'Well,' he said, as she bent to kiss his cheek, 'you're looking a great deal better, if I'm to believe what Janet's been telling me.'

Robyn smiled. 'Tactful as ever,' she remarked, taking the seat across from him. 'I've just had a shower and washed my hair, that's all. I felt like smartening myself up. Do you mind?'

'Why should I mind?' retorted Ben irascibly. 'I'm just the resident geriatric here, that's all. Nobody tells me anything. I'm not considered intelligent enough to understand the simplest problem!'

Robyn's smile disappeared. 'That's not true, Ben——'

'It is true.' He sniffed. 'Anyway, how are you feeling? I could say, I told you so, but I don't suppose you'd want to hear it.'

'Ben——'

'Well, at least that fool, Kingsley, hasn't been pestering us again since Janet gave him his marching orders.'

'Ben!'

'Now, don't look like that.' Ben grimaced. 'I had Jared send a sizeable contribution to the vicar's favourite charity, so I don't suppose old Tomlinson will be complaining.'

'Even so...'

'Even so, nothing. No wishy-washy curate is good enough for my daughter-in-law, no matter how attractive he might be. Even if she does treat me like an imbecile, she's family. And whatever her faults, that's the important thing.'

Robyn sighed. 'Ben, I realise you think I've been deceiving you——'

'Damn right!'

'—but it's not true.' She sighed, searching for the right words to tell him how she felt. 'I—I wasn't sure. I wasn't certain I was right. It wasn't until—until——'

'—until Jared had the sense to see through Woodhouse's lies!' snapped Ben harshly. 'I know, I know. He's told me all about it. At least he still thinks I've got a brain in my head!'

'Oh, Ben——'

'What I can't understand is how Stephen didn't notice what was going on,' the old man continued, and Robyn's features froze. 'Still, I suppose he never was much of an accountant, was he? And a clever man like Maurice Woodhouse—well, I reckon he must have run rings around him.'

Robyn caught her breath. 'Stephen—didn't—know?' she ventured faintly, and her father-in-law shook his head.

'Well, it stands to reason, doesn't it? Stephen would have told me if he'd noticed anything amiss. But Jared says Woodhouse must have been too sneaky for him, and if, as he says, there was a second set of books——'

Robyn was breathing shallowly now, and it wasn't easy to hide her reaction from the old man. She couldn't believe what she was hearing; she couldn't believe Maurice Woodhouse had been prepared to take all the blame; it didn't gell with what she knew of him. And, in any case, Jared had known the truth and had intended to act upon it.

'Thank God Jared came home when he did,' Ben was saying now. 'Although I'm not sure I entirely agree with the way he's handling it.'

Robyn swallowed. 'No?' she managed croakily.

'No.' Ben gnawed at his lower lip. 'You see, he's got some fool notion that a scandal at this time could do more harm to the company than it would to Maurice Woodhouse. He's an old man, like myself; he's near to retiring. There's no doubt that he'd go to prison if it got

out, but Jared reckons it's not worth it for the satisfaction it would give us.'

'I see.' Robyn nodded.

'Well?' Ben gazed at her impatiently, and when she
didn't immediately respond he added sharply, 'What do
you think? What's your opinion? As acting managing
director of Morley Textiles, you ought to have an
opinion.'

Robyn swallowed again. 'Um—oh, I agree with Jared,'
she got out in a little rush. 'That is—it does seem more
sensible not to—not to rock the boat.'

'Huh!' Ben snorted. 'I suppose I should have expected
that. Women! They always take the easy way out. Oh,
well, if that's your decision, I'll go along with it. I don't
have much choice, do I? But I'll tell you one thing,
Robyn, Stephen wouldn't have let him get away with it.
Not Stephen. He was too much like me!'

Jared came to bed at about half-past eleven. Robyn heard
him come upstairs. She had been listening for him. Even
if she hadn't, she was sure she would have sensed it in
her present state of tension. She had been wanting to
talk to him alone all evening, ever since he and Daniel
got back from Sheffield. But for once he had proved
annoyingly elusive. Despite several thwarted efforts, she
had had no opportunity to say what she wanted to say,
and she had begun to wonder if he was deliberately
avoiding her.

She had stayed up for supper, even though Janet had
expressed the view that she might be overdoing things
by doing so. But she had been sure that, at some point
in the evening, she would get Jared on his own, and her
frustration had known no bounds when her son proved
to be the obstacle. Allowed to stay up for supper because of his mother, Daniel had succeeded in monopolising the conversation both during and after the meal.
He had entertained his grandfather by recounting every
minute of his day in Sheffield, even telling him about

the cars, and the multi-storey car park, and the self-service cafeteria where they had had their lunch.

By the time the meal was over, Robyn's nerves were stretched as taut as violin strings and, when Janet eventually offered to take her son away to bed, she had held her breath. But, although Jared had often said goodnight to Daniel after he was tucked up, tonight he didn't. Instead, he said he was going to have a nightcap with his father, and Daniel had to be content with a promise to take him riding the next day. 'If your mother doesn't object, of course,' Jared had added, with an un-smiling glance in Robyn's direction. 'He does have a pony, doesn't he? And the roads around the estate are fairly dry.'

In consequence of which, Robyn had said her good-nights, too, and gone to bed. But not to sleep. For the past two and a half hours, she had been lying awake, wondering if she dared intercept Jared on his way to bed. In the event, she heard the door of his room close while she was still considering her options, and the silence of the house seemed to mock her good intentions.

With an exclamation of impatience, she came to a de-cision. Jared hadn't had time yet to get undressed, and there was no way she was going to sleep without speaking to him first. She had to know what he had said to his father; she had to thank him, if thanks were adequate, for what he had done for Daniel. How he had succeeded in keeping Stephen's name out of the accusations, she couldn't imagine, but somehow he had done it, and she had to tell him she was grateful.

Sliding out of bed, she slipped her feet into furry mules and reached for her dressing-gown. Its dark red velour folds were warm from lying across the foot of her bed, and she cast a rueful glance at her reflection in the mirror before opening the bedroom door. So much for the ef-forts she had made with her appearance, she thought wryly. Now, without make-up, and with her hair pulled back into a single braid, she had no delusions of glamour, but perhaps that was just as well. The last thing she wanted was for Jared to get the wrong impression.

As she had expected, a ribbon of light showed beneath the bottom of Jared's door; summoning all her confidence, she knocked lightly on the panels. Then, she waited, her fists balling in the pockets of her dressing-gown, endeavouring to marshall all she wanted to say, without giving away either her nervousness or her feelings.

As on that other unforgettable occasion when she had come to his room, Jared didn't immediately respond to her summons. On the contrary, she was obliged to knock again before she attracted his attention, and she was glad Daniel's apartments were at the other end of the corridor.

However, much to her relief, when Jared did open the door, he was still fully clothed. He had shed the black suede jacket he had worn to supper, but he was still dressed in matching trousers, and a beige silk shirt. And, although the cuffs of his shirt were folded back over his forearms, most of his tanned brown skin was hidden from her gaze.

'Well, well,' he said, with just a faint edge to his voice. 'Surprise, surprise! Why did I know it would be you? Could it be because there's nobody else in the house?'

Robyn moistened her lips. 'That's not true——'

'No.' He conceded the point with an inclination of his head. 'Mac and Janet are in their flat downstairs, and my father is asleep in his ground-floor apartments. Oh— I suppose it could have been Dan, but somehow I didn't think so.'

Robyn let him finish, and then she said quietly, 'Can I come in?'

'In here?' Jared arched a mocking brow. 'Is that wise? You know what happened the last time. Aren't you afraid that I might compromise you?'

Robyn sighed. 'Must you be so sarcastic?'

'Perhaps I feel sarcastic,' retorted Jared shortly. And then, meeting her troubled stare, he made a frustrated gesture. 'Of course, of course. Come in, why don't you?

It wouldn't do for anyone to see us. They might get the wrong impression.'

Robyn stepped past him as he stood aside, and then took a few steps more as he closed the door behind her. Curiously enough, she didn't feel at all nervous now she was here, though she suspected her confidence could evaporate if Jared chose to take the advantage.

'So,' he said, walking past her and halting at the end of his bed. He folded his arms, and waited. 'I assume this visit has a purpose. It's not just a—social call.'

Robyn straightened her spine. 'I suppose you can guess why I'm here.'

'Maybe.' He was non-committal. 'Suppose you tell me.'

Robyn caught her lower lip between her teeth. 'I wanted to thank you. For—for keeping Stephen's name out of the trouble at Morley's. I don't know how you did it, but Daniel and I will never be able to thank you enough.'

Jared shrugged. 'I didn't do it for you. I did it for my father. He's had enough shocks lately. One more might have killed him.'

Robyn nodded. 'Of course. But—even so——'

'Forget it.' Jared was dismissive. 'It was no big deal. Woodhouse was pathetically eager to save his own hide. He'd have done anything to avoid going to prison.'

'But—he is leaving, isn't he?'

'He's taking an early retirement.'

'And won't that cause some talk?'

'I shouldn't think so.' Jared was laconic. 'He's an old man. He's been seeing a doctor about high blood pressure for some time. It'll look perfectly natural. Even if it was probably aggravated by the stress of what they were doing.'

Robyn expelled her breath slowly. 'Thank God!'

'For what? Saving Stephen's memory?' Jared looked scornful. 'That's not something that gives me any pleasure. But, if it makes you happy, then so be it. And at least Dan doesn't have to know anything about it.'

Robyn hesitated. 'You really—care about him, don't you?'

'Dan?' Jared's lips twisted. 'I suppose you think I'm a fool, hmm?'

'No!'

'No?'

'No, why should I?'

'Because he's not my son.'

Robyn caught her breath. 'Does that matter. You're still his uncle.'

'It matters,' said Jared heavily, turning away. 'But it doesn't alter my feelings for him, if that's what you mean.'

Robyn licked her lips. 'I'm glad.'

'Are you?' Jared looked at her over his shoulder, his expression sceptical. 'Just so long as he's not mine, you don't mind if I care about him. When you thought he was my son, you couldn't bear me to be near him.'

'That's not how it was.' Robyn gazed at him unhappily. 'I—I was afraid. Afraid of what you might do to him.'

Jared swung back to face her again. 'What I might *do* to him? What the hell do you mean?'

'Oh——' Robyn shook her head. 'You don't understand.'

'No, I bloody don't!'

'I'm expressing myself badly.' Robyn made a helpless gesture. 'I thought you might try to—to take him away from me. I thought if you knew he was yours, you might take me to court to prove it.'

Jared looked aghast. 'Why in God's name would you think a thing like that?' He shook his head. 'Did I ever threaten you?'

'No.'

'Did I ever give you any reason to think I might take legal steps to prove myself his father?'

'No.'

'Then what the——'

'You wouldn't leave me alone!' burst out Robyn painfully. 'When—when you saw you weren't getting anywhere by normal means, you started coming on to me. You—you pretended you cared about me, just to get me to admit that Daniel was yours!'

Jared swore then, his face contorted with emotion. 'You—fool!' he muttered. 'You crazy little fool! Do you really think I'd marry you just to claim my rights as Dan's father?'

Robyn quivered. 'Well—I thought—that is, when you came back——'

'Oh, I know.' Jared remembered. 'When I came home, I let you think I hated you. Perhaps I did hate you then. I certainly hated you when I went away. When you had the baby and I thought he was mine, I think I wanted to kill you!'

Robyn swallowed. 'I'm sorry.'

'Yes. So was I.' Jared spoke bitterly. 'But that's all water under the bridge now, as they say, isn't it? What's past is gone, and you don't have to be afraid of me any more,' he finished sardonically.

Robyn held up her head. 'I'm not afraid of you.'

'Not now,' jeered Jared scornfully.

'All right. Not now.' Robyn drew her hands out of her pockets and linked them together. 'As—as a matter of fact, I think I love you.' She paused. 'Is it too late to tell you that? Will you even believe me?'

Jared uttered a choking sound. 'What did you say?' he demanded, staring at her as if she had taken leave of her senses, and Robyn wondered if she had made a terrible mistake.

Clearing her throat, as if the obstruction had been hers, she said, 'I think you heard me,' in low uneven tones. 'I—love you. I think I always have. But you were so much younger than me, and I dared not take the chance that you might change your mind.'

Jared blinked. 'And—what makes you think I might not change my mind now?' he asked in a strangled voice. 'I mean—you are still older than me, aren't you? And, as you pointed out earlier, I do have proof now that Dan's *not* my son.'

Robyn trembled slightly, but she held her ground. 'You—you said you wouldn't marry me just to claim your rights as Daniel's father.'

Jared inclined his head. 'So I did.'

'Well, then?'

'Well, then, what?'

Robyn fists clenched. 'Jared!'

'Did I ask you to marry me?' he asked infuriatingly. 'I'm sorry, I don't remember that.'

Robyn stared at him for a moment longer, and then her shoulders sagged. 'I see.'

'What do you see, I wonder?' Jared's voice was rough now, and the mockery he had exhibited moments before had completely disappeared. 'You have a nerve, do you know that? For the past few weeks you've treated me like dirt, telling me things you didn't believe to be true, and making me feel like an intruder in my own home!'

'That's not true!'

'A favourite cry of yours, but it *is* true, Robyn! You did your best to turn Dan against me——'

'No!'

'—and you rejected every move I made towards you.'

'You know why!' she exclaimed defensively.

'I know what you've told me,' retorted Jared, a muscle jerking at the corner of his mouth. 'But now, how do I know you're not just approaching me because of Dan, hmm? I mean, now that he's not my son, perhaps you're afraid I'll not make him my heir?'

Robyn gasped. 'I—I would never do such a thing!'

'Wouldn't you?'

'You know I wouldn't.' She shook her head. 'That—that's a foul thing to suggest!'

'No worse than what you accused me of, remember?' Jared reminded her harshly. 'How do you like it, Robyn? How do you like being made to feel a louse?'

Robyn shook her head. And then, moving a little dazedly, she turned towards the door. 'I'm sorry,' she said, swallowing back the lump of emotion that seemed to have balled in her throat as he spoke. 'I—er—I seem to have made a mistake. I'm sorry. I'll leave you now. I shouldn't have come——'

'Oh, for Christ's sake!' Before she could reach the door, Jared moved after her, his hands capturing her arms and halting her progress. 'You're not going anywhere,' he added, the warmth of his breathing stirring the hairs on the back of her neck. 'All right, it was cruel, but I had to do it. You've hurt me so many times, don't you think I deserve a little restitution?'

Robyn bent her head. 'What do you mean?' she asked in a small voice, and Jared uttered a self-derisive laugh as he pulled her back against him.

'Don't push your luck,' he advised, his lips soft against the side of her neck. 'You know what I mean. I mean I'm fool enough to forgive you anything. Even ruining eight years of our lives, just to prove I really knew what I was doing.'

Robyn's breathing quickened. 'Do you mean it?' she asked huskily, tilting her head to facilitate his caressing exploration of her nape. She felt his rueful amusement whisper against her skin.

'Would I lie to you?' he demanded, turning her to face him. And then, cupping her face in his hands, he added, 'Does this mean you will marry me, as soon as a decent interval has elapsed?'

'If that's what you want.' Robyn covered his hands with her own.

'It's what I want,' Jared confirmed, stroking his lips against hers. 'It's what I've always wanted. So long as this isn't some misguided sense of gratitude because Steve is off the hook.'

'Oh, Jared!' With a cry of protest, she wound her arms round his neck, bringing his mouth hard to hers and sliding her tongue between his lips. 'Does this feel like gratitude?' she panted, when they were both weak and short of breath, and Jared gave a muffled oath as he swung her up into his arms.

'At least you came ready for bed,' he teased softly, setting her down on his own quilt, and rapidly tearing off his shirt and tie. 'Although I don't think much of this nightshirt,' he appended, growing impatient with the neat row of buttons that confronted him. With a groan of impatience, he snapped the buttons from their holes and sent half a dozen of them tumbling on to the floor. 'Mmm, that's much better,' he approved, lowering his face into the hollow between her breasts. 'Ah, Robyn, Robyn,' he breathed, 'how I love you! Will you believe me now if I tell you that this is the most wonderful Christmas gift of all?'

It was in July of the following year that Robyn discovered she was expecting Jared's baby.

There was no mistake this time. She and her husband had been married for almost three months, and, although some people had expressed the opinion that six months was an inordinately short period of mourning, most had approved the match and offered their congratulations. Anyone who had known Stephen, and the humiliating existence Robyn had led with him, was more than willing to give them their good wishes. And everyone, without exception, applauded her choice, for Jared had always inspired the most affection.

For Robyn, the past six months had been the happiest six months of her whole life. Ben was happy, Daniel was happy, and she was happy, undeservedly so, she sometimes thought, considering the way she had almost ruined both hers and Jared's lives.

But, as to that, she was doing her best to make up for all the years she had wasted, and she knew she was succeeding. Jared had never looked more attractive or more content, and she knew he was happy, too, because he never ceased convincing her.

Even so, it was quite a traumatic prospect, to tell Jared he was going to be a father at last. She didn't quite know how he would take it, particularly as they had originally agreed that they should not have any children for the first couple of years.

'We'll let Dan get used to having a new father first,' Jared had suggested gently. 'I know he likes me, and I don't think he minds us getting married. But coping with a new half-brother or sister—well, let's take it one step at a time, shall we? We can wait. We've got all the rest of our lives.'

And they did. And just being together had proved to be all she could ever have wished. Their honeymoon— a week in Venice, which was all the time Jared could take away from the business—might not have been as glamorous as the honeymoon in the Bahamas she had spent with Stephen, but it had been so much more enviable. In spite of the fact that April had proved to be rather a chilly month, with the occasional downpour for good measure, Robyn and Jared had scarcely noticed. They had spent most of their time alone in the splendid isolation of the suite Jared had booked for them at the Danieli Hotel, and only the pealing bells from the city's many *campaniles* reminded them where they were. Oh, they had done a little sightseeing, and Jared had taken her for a romantic ride on a gondola. But mostly they were content to spend their time together, and Robyn knew they attracted many smiles from the friendly, sentimental Italians.

In consequence, Robyn broached the subject of her pregnancy with some reluctance. What if Jared didn't want a child? What if he was quite content as Daniel's stepfather? Would he still love her when she became bloated and ungainly? Had she made a terrible mistake by not taking care that it didn't happen?

Daniel was the first person she encountered when she got home from the doctor's. He was playing in the garden with the puppy Jared had bought him for his birthday, and Robyn saw with some misgivings that one of them had trampled all over Janet's herb garden. Oh, well, she thought resignedly, the McClouds had been as keen as

Daniel to buy the young Dalmation, and Janet was perfectly capable of chastising him for herself.

Daniel himself looked fit and healthy. Since Jared's advent into his life, he had joined the local cub pack, and rode regularly with his stepfather. Jared was even talking about getting him a bigger pony at Christmas, and Robyn was really delighted that they got on so well together.

It had been Jared's suggestion, too, that they abandon all ideas of sending Daniel away to school until he was at least thirteen. The prep school he attended had an excellent reputation and, as neither she nor Jared wanted him to go away, it was a very satisfactory arrangement. Besides, they were a real family now, and Robyn had seen her son's growing confidence since Jared came into his life.

Now, he followed her indoors, poking into the shopping bag she set down in the hall, and begging a chocolate biscuit that he found there. 'You've been a long time,' he said, accompanying her into the sitting-room and flinging himself on to one of the pair of sofas that faced one another across the hearth. 'Grandpa said you had an appointment at the doctor's. Did you? *Did you*?'

Robyn was glad she could be truthful. 'I had to go and get a prescription for your grandfather's new tablets,' she said, producing the bottle she had got from the chemist's from her handbag. She remembered that other occasion Dr Harrington had asked to see her to discuss her father-in-law's medication. That was when she had accused Jared of spying on her. How foolish she had been then.

'Is that all?'

Daniel's voice interrupted her reverie and she sighed. 'Well, I had to get the prescription filled, and there were one or two other things I had to buy.'

'Like these biscuits,' agreed Daniel enthusiastically, peeling off the wrapper and taking a bite. 'A pity. I thought there might have been another reason for you

to see the doctor. Lester—one of the chaps at school—
his mother's going to have a baby, and I know she goes
to see the doctor regularly.'

Robyn managed to hide her start of surprise. 'And—
would you like that?' she ventured tentatively. 'If I had
a baby, I mean?'

'Well, I think so.' Daniel grimaced. 'I wouldn't like
its crying, of course, but they don't do that all the time,
do they?'

'No...'

'And it's quite natural, isn't it?' Daniel continued. 'I
mean, you and Uncle Jared—that is, *Dad*—are married,
aren't you? And married people do have babies. I was
really quite expecting it.'

Robyn decided to tell Jared her news while he was
taking a bath that same evening. He usually left the
bathroom door open while he was in the tub, and Robyn
positioned herself just beyond the door so she wouldn't
have to look at him when she said it.

'Jared?' she called, pressing her shoulders back against
the wall of their bedroom. 'I've got something to tell
you.'

'I've got something to tell you, too,' remarked Jared,
and Robyn's brows drew together uncertainly.

'You do?'

'Yes.' She heard him sigh. 'Look, why don't you come
in here, hmm? To save me having to shout at you. I
thought you were going to take a shower.'

Robyn caught her breath. 'I was.'

'Well, then?'

She hesitated. 'In a minute.'

There was a sudden movement from the bath, and the
swoosh as water overspilled the tub, but before Robyn
could anticipate what he was doing Jared appeared in
the bedroom doorway. He was in the process of drying
himself as he came, and the soft folds of a creamy apricot
towel half covered his chest and were caught between
the muscular strength of his thighs. He looked so attractive at that moment, his blond hair artificially

darkened by the water, and his body still tanned several shades darker except below his waist, that Robyn wanted to go to him and wrap her arms around him. But what she had to tell him had to be said and, subduing her instincts, she turned away from the sensual beauty of his physique.

'I'm—pregnant,' she said, her nervous fingers busy with the ribbons of the silky beige teddy she was wearing. Still without looking at him, she bent to pick up a stocking she had discarded earlier and threaded it through her hands like a lifeline. Realising several seconds had gone by and he had not said anything, she was compelled to find out why and, turning her head again, she added, 'I know we didn't plan it, but—well, are you mad?'

Jared threw the towel into the bathroom behind him. 'Are you?'

Robyn lifted her slim shoulders. 'Why should I be?'

'That's not an answer.'

'Nor was yours,' she countered unevenly, forcing herself not to dwell on his lean powerful body. 'If—if there's a problem——'

Jared uttered an expletive. 'Why should there be?'

'Oh——' Robyn made a helpless gesture. 'Oh—you're making me nervous, Jared. I knew this wasn't going to be easy. That was why I wanted to get it over with.'

'By shouting it from the bedroom,' observed Jared flatly.

Robyn shrugged. 'Perhaps.' She glanced his way briefly, and then away again. 'Um—oughtn't you to put some clothes on? You'll get cold.' She paused. 'What was it you wanted to tell me?'

'Later,' said Jared, abandoning his stance by the door and coming towards her. 'Now, come on,' he said, pulling her away from the wall and into his arms. 'What's your problem, hmm? Don't you want another baby, is that it? Or are you afraid Daniel might object?'

Robyn linked her arms around his neck, gazing up at him with anxious eyes. 'I don't have a problem—not with the baby, anyway,' she admitted huskily. 'And, as far as Daniel is concerned, he told me this afternoon he was disappointed I wasn't pregnant.'

'So did you enlighten him?'

'No.' Robyn was indignant. 'No one knows but you.'

'And I'm your problem?'

Robyn bent her head, pressing her forehead against his chest. 'I don't know.'

'What don't you know?' Jared's voice roughened as he put his fingers beneath her chin and tilted her face upward. 'Surely you don't really believe I wouldn't be delighted? My God, Robyn, I can think of nothing more exciting than the prospect of you carrying my child inside you. So long as that's what you want, I want it, too.'

'But you said——'

'Yes, what did I say?'

'Well—I thought you wanted to wait.'

'I thought that was what *you* wanted,' admitted Jared roughly. 'After—after everything that had gone before, I didn't want to rush you. I didn't want you to think I'd married you just to have my child.'

'Oh.'

'Is that all you can say? Oh?'

Robyn bit her lip. 'You won't mind when I get fat and ugly?'

'You may get fat, but you'll never be ugly to me,' retorted Jared.

'But I will get big—and clumsy——'

'And I'll love you just the same. Now, stop fishing for compliments.'

'I'm not.' Robyn hesitated. 'All right. Tell me what you wanted to say, then.'

Jared pulled a wry face. 'Would you believe I was going to tell you that I'm planning to expand, too? I'm going to buy the land next to the mill and put up another weaving shed.'

'Oh!' Robyn dimpled. 'How appropriate!'

'But now,' he said huskily, pressing a kiss to the corner of her mouth, 'now I'm going to finish my bath.'

She gasped when he swung her up into his arms then, and carried her into the bathroom. 'What are you doing?' she exclaimed, when he deposited her, still in her teddy, in the bath of soapy water.

'I'm taking a bath—and you—at the same time,' responded Jared, stepping into the deep round tub with her. Then, peeling the wet straps of her bodice down off her shoulders, he covered her mouth with his, sinking down into the water with her and pulling her fully against him.

'I—we can't!' moaned Robyn, feeling the lacy teddy floating around somewhere near her hips, but his touch was unbearably exciting and it was only a token protest.

'Of course we can,' he murmured thickly, his hands busy under the water. Seconds later, the teddy floated away, removing the last barrier. 'My wife, my mistress, my lover,' he breathed softly. 'And the mother of my children. What more could any man ask?'

Step into a world of pulsing adventure, gripping emotion and lush sensuality with these evocative love stories penned by today's best-selling authors in the highest romantic tradition. Pursuing their passionate dreams against a backdrop of the past's most colorful and dramatic moments, our vibrant heroines and dashing heroes will make history come alive for you.

Watch for two new Harlequin Historicals each month, available wherever Harlequin books are sold. History was never so much fun—you won't want to miss a single moment!

Harlequin American Romance

Romances that go one step farther...
American Romance

Realistic stories involving people you can relate to and care about.

Compelling relationships between the mature men and women of today's world.

Romances that capture the core of genuine emotions between a man and a woman.

Join us each month for four new titles wherever paperback books are sold.
Enter the world of American Romance.

Harlequin Romance

Enter the world of Romance...
Harlequin Romance

Delight in the exotic yet innocent love stories of
Harlequin Romance.

Be whisked away to dazzling international capitals...or
quaint European villages.

Experience the joys of falling in love...for the first
time, the best time!

Six new titles every month for your reading enjoyment.
Available wherever paperbacks are sold.